CW00517265

FAIR MEANS OR FOUL?

FAIR MEANS OR FOUL?

FRED GEE

KAMA PUBLICATIONS

FAIR MEANS OR FOUL?

First Published by Kama Publications
Kama, Belaugh, Norfolk NR12 8UX

© Fred Gee 2001

ISBN 0 953 6355 1 1

All rights reserved. Apart from fair dealing for the purposes of study, research, criticism or review, as permitted under the Copyright Designs and Patents Act, 1998, no part of this publication may be reproduced, stored in a retrieval system, or transmitted in any form or by any means, electronic, electrical, chemical, mechanical, photocopying, recording or otherwise without the prior permission of the copyright owners. Enquiries should be addressed to the publishers.

Produced and printed in England by
Barnwell's Print Ltd
Barnwell's Printing Works
Penfold Street, Aylsham
Norfolk NR11 6ET

Cover illustration by Gill Baguley

Dedication

*To all surviving village shopkeepers,
and those who continue to shop with them.*

Chapter 1

When people in the village of Backwater were told that Bernard and his wife would be taking over the *General Stores*, they were assured they would get the same service and satisfaction as when Harry and Mildred were running it. One by one they now seemed intent on putting that to the test.

'Your father always gave me an extra pennyworth, for luck,' said one old lady who looked as though she had a knack of organising her own good fortune.

'I suppose the shop was getting too much for your poor mother,' said another lady looking considerably older than Bernard's parent. 'I daresay it will soon be too much for me to get here.' Bernard guessed there was a motive for that remark and offered to deliver her goods in future. 'Oh no, I couldn't let you do that, Mr Talbot, I always want to see what I'm getting before I buy anything!'

'Don't suppose you remember me, young Bernie?' said a grey haired gentleman leaning on a walking stick. 'You used t'nick apples from my garden when you thought I weren't lookin'. Better watch out I don't get me own back now you're goin' to be sellin' `em!'

Backwater, as its name suggests, was a small hamlet in a county that included settlements with such unlikely names as Sloley, and Seething, and Snoring. It was virtually unknown even to its closest neighbours, and you will not find it in any authentic atlas.

The Talbots, on the other hand, were the kind of family which might be found anywhere in England. Bernard was an amiable husband, thoughtful, helpful and optimistic by nature; Cynthia a sensible wife, practical but prone to occasional bouts of pessimism. Contented, if not always happy, they were proud of the two children they were bringing up.

Bernard had been brought up in Backwater but broke away when he was old enough to earn a living. Cynthia grew up in an urban environment and was totally unfamiliar with the country.

Nothing in Bernard's experience since leaving school had prepared him for life as a shopkeeper, and he had not expected to inherit the *Stores* while his father and mother were still alive. He had been making his way in the world as a bank clerk with the modest, if uninspiring, ambition of one day becoming a bank manager. He was now a proficient collector and dispenser of money, but having to sell something in order to produce it seemed a risky and arduous business by comparison. He was not to know that by the time he would be ready to achieve his ambition the position of bank manager would no longer exist. Realistically it seemed he had no option but to take over the shop and move back to the country. A family tradition had already been established. His grandfather had passed the business on to his father, and he was his father's only son.

Cynthia, however, saw things differently. She was not at all sure that she wanted to forego the comfort of a newly built suburban bungalow for the cramped conditions of an ancient house in the country. Moreover, she knew that one of the ground floor rooms of that house had been adapted to create the shop. She thought of the house as a convenient holiday home but dreaded the prospect of living there permanently.

In the days that followed she brought forward a succession of arguments to counter her husband's readiness to move.

'We'd miss the cinema, you know,' she said.
'When did we last go to a cinema?'
'And there won't be a Public Library....'
'When did you last read a book?'
'Well, we'll certainly miss all the shops.'
'What do you mean? We'll have one of our own!'

Cynthia next wondered if they would have room to accommodate all their furniture and still have space to spare for the shop.

'There are more rooms in that house than we have in the bungalow,' said Bernard.

'Yes, but they're all smaller, and differently shaped.'

Bernard drew breath, but could not deny it.

'And, there's another drawback,' she added. 'The living room leads directly on to the shop and the public can see straight in when the door is open.'

'Don't worry,' said Bernard, 'that will only happen during working hours when we'll not be using it.'

Cynthia remembered the children: Jonathan aged nine, and Amy seven.

'They've got rooms next to ours in the bungalow....'

'They'll still have a room each,' said their father, '- upstairs, out of earshot!'

'What about their education?'

'There'll be my old school,' said Bernard, 'until they're ten. After that there's the county school, which has a better reputation nowadays than when I was there.'

Cynthia missed the irony and continued to agonise. 'They'll have a lot further to go though, won't they?'

'Maybe, but I'd rather they grew up in the country where the air is less polluted.'

'Bernard, really! Did you never go near a pigsty?'

The debate continued as Cynthia thought of more and more reasons why they ought not to move to the country, and it was not until Bernard promised to sell up and move again if life became intolerable that her resistance was overcome.

The day of the move was typically traumatic. Pickfords' men reached the bungalow early, before Cynthia was ready for them, and insisted on helping her with last-minute packing. This meant she was unable to label everything for where she thought it should go. Halfway through the morning it rained. One of the removal men slipped on the pavement and dropped a load of ornaments, much to the amusement of the children who were watching from a neighbour's window. Happily, they were well packed and none of them was broken but it added to Cynthia's mood of foreboding.

Once the bungalow was empty Cynthia insisted on staying behind to make sure nothing had been overlooked, and to remove any cobwebs or stains on the woodwork. Bernard rode with the removal van to Backwater where he was greeted with cups of tea by his mother and keys to the shop by his father. His parents' belongings had meantime been moved to a cottage elsewhere in the village.

By the time Cynthia reached the shop all her chattels had been unloaded and the removal men were sitting at the foot of the stairs, exhausted. Lifting wardrobes into the upstairs bedrooms, via a steep staircase and narrow landing, had taken longer and caused more sweat than moving them out of the bungalow. They were glad Cynthia had not been around to change her mind, or listen to their expletives.

That night the whole family sat together in the living room with the door to the shop firmly shut, and drank a toast to their future. Bernard's mother cried a little, because she said she would miss the happy days they had spent in the *General Stores*, even while there was a war on. His father laughed and said he believed no-one in the village knew there had been a war on! Bernard confessed that his boyhood memories of living in the village had mostly faded but said he would not forget harvest time in the cornfields when he chased rabbits as they ran for cover from the cutters. Cynthia asked if he ever chased girls in the cornfields, but his father answered for him by saying none of the girls in the village would have run for cover!

His mother's tears of laughter at her husband's teasing soon changed to melancholy as she recalled her lifetime in the shop. She knew all her customers by name and they knew her as Mildred, or in some cases Milly. She kept a chair in front of the counter for the weary or chatty, and in the days before everyone had a radio or television set a regular news service emanated from the *General Stores*. Very little happened in the village that she and her husband were not aware of, or did not pass on in the course of conversation. Their only rivals in the communication business were the church and public house, and they catered for different needs.

As Cynthia listened to the conversation she doubted yet again if such a lifestyle would make *her* happy. The atmosphere in the cottage was heavy and the wine was going to her head. Without tact or apology, she asked her mother-in-law why she wanted to give it all up.

It was a cathartic moment. There was a long silence and the mood changed.

'We've had to cope with a lot of problems,' said Mildred. 'So many new commodities have been coming on to the market recently it's been difficult keeping up with them. People of our age want to buy what they're familiar with, but younger folk want what's new. We've tried to meet demand but it's meant cramming more stock on shelves and then having to remember where we put them. Besides, neither of us is getting any younger, and ...'

Harry interrupted. 'We did our best, but when they brought in decimal currency, it all became too much and we decided it was time to retire.'

Next morning Bernard and Cynthia had the shop to themselves.

The first few days were difficult. Everywhere and everything was strange. Not only had they to find their way among unfamiliar goods for a queue of curious customers but they also had to cope with the old-fashioned machinery still being used to cash in money and weigh out the goods. There were brass weights and boat-shaped pans for measuring modest quantities and spring

4

scales for large and heavy items. Payment was always in cash, because credit cards had yet to be invented, and money was stacked away beneath the counter in a shallow wooden box. It was a far cry from the bank where Bernard had worked, or the market where Cynthia had done her shopping.

Bernard found the experience of dealing with customers across an open counter somewhat alarming, but less so than filling their baskets and answering their questions. Cynthia was never too proud to admit she had a lot to learn, and the villagers were ever ready to teach her what they thought she ought to know.

There is an old saying that two cooks in the same kitchen do not make good workmates. Bernard and Cynthia soon found themselves quarrelling about how best to arrange the goods on shelves and floor-space. Loyal to his parents, Bernard wanted to leave everything where it was and put replacement stocks where the old stock had been, but Cynthia wanted to create a more logical distribution.

'We've only been here five minutes,' said Bernard, 'so how do you know where *is* best to keep them?'

'The ones that people ask for most often ought to be close to hand.'

'Wouldn't it be better to wait until we do a stock-take?'

'The stock-take will be easier to carry out if we've put everything in a sensible order first. '

'OK. So, where do we start? And when?'

'How about now, with all those jars of unsold humbugs!'

Bernard wanted to say *humbug,* but thought better of it.

'Of course they're unsold, or they wouldn't be there, would they?'

'When I moved the jar this morning the sweets were stuck together like peas in a glue-pot! I doubt if anyone here has bought a humbug for years.'

When Bernard suggested to Cynthia that they might do what his parents had done and take turns in the shop according to who is available, rather than have any fixed arrangement, Cynthia disagreed.

'I'd prefer to be methodical,' she said, 'then we'll know where we stand. I suggest you work in the shop in the mornings while I'm doing the housework; then I'll come in for the afternoons while you do the paperwork and deliveries.'

What Cynthia had overlooked was that Harry and Mildred often kept the shop open until late at night and at weekends and public holidays, creating a legend that the *General Stores* never closed.

This had not bothered Harry or Mildred who never took holidays, rarely left home to relax, and habitually sat or ate in the living room with the door to the shop wide open. It did, however, bother Bernard and Cynthia. They valued their privacy and missed the opportunities for outside entertainment which they once enjoyed. They underestimated the extent to which they would be tied to the business. It was all very well drawing up a schedule to apportion the work, but they soon realised that if either of them became sick, or had an accident, the other one would be left to operate the shop alone. Traditional holidays with the children would be a thing of the past, as would the idea of a weekend break. Many jobs could only be done when the shop was closed. Amy offered to help her mother in the house and often did so when not at school or doing homework, but Jonathan made it very clear to his father that he was not interested in becoming a shopkeeper. He had no wish, he said, to inherit the family business when it was his turn for this to happen.

Bernard was disappointed but remembered his own indifference to the idea when he was Jonathan's age.

'We could, of course, ask my father and mother to come back for a few days to help out occasionally,' he suggested.

'I think not,' said Cynthia. 'It would lead to unpleasantness once they found how much we had altered from the way it used to be.

'Very well, then, we'll ask my Aunt Violet.'

'Over my dead body!' said Cynthia. 'She would put everything back the way it used to be!'

Chapter 2

It was not only the management of the village shop and the goods which were sold there that had changed. Life in the village was changing. New people were moving in from urban areas and a younger generation was growing up with likes and dislikes that differed from those of the older inhabitants. Their habits and manners were different; they wore different clothes and hairstyles. The only thing that remained reasonably constant was the shape and nature of the countryside. For hundreds of years one generation had succeeded another within broadly the same environment, so that sons and daughters grew up to a background that was entirely familiar to their parents. This was no longer the case. Newspapers, films and television provided a platform on which youth built and developed a separate culture. Ideas and fashions that had satisfied their elders were debunked and devalued. Young people were earning more than ever before and many of them had money to spare for what their parents would have regarded as luxuries.

The residents of Backwater were not yet subjected to all the distractions and wonders of modern technology that were available to city-dwellers, but they were no less influenced in the way they spent their time and money by what they saw each night on television. For some it meant closer relationships within the family as they huddled together in front of their receiver but in others it encouraged arguments and alienation as they quarrelled over their choice of programmes and entertainers. Commercially, it meant loss of business to the publican, until he learned to fix a screen in sight of the bar, and to Bernard and Cynthia it meant more goods being sold of the kind that had recently featured in a televised advertisement.

For a long time Cynthia continued to stock what she believed to be items of established popularity, only to find as the months passed that many of them remained on the shelves unsold. Meanwhile, Bernard on his delivery rounds was frequently asked for products he had never heard of until his children told him 'they were advertised on the telly.' As a result the shop rapidly ran out of shelving space.

'Can't you find somewhere else to keep those tins of peas?'

'Must you order those new-fangled bottles of washing-up liquid? No-one in the village will ever buy them.'

The clamour for new products soon overtook the rate at which Cynthia reduced her stock of slow-moving items and Bernard was forced to find more room to display the ever increasing variety of goods on offer. He turned his attention to the art of marketing.

'We'll have to make more use of the front window.'

'What, and let people see into our living quarters?'

'We could put a curtain up in front of the door to the living room.'

'Then we wouldn't know when there was a customer in the shop.'

'We'll put a bell on the front door so it rings when the door opens.'

'What about in the summer when we keep the front door open all the time?'

'We'll put a bell on the counter.'

'Suppose they don't ring it! How do we stop people helping themselves if we don't know they're in the shop?'

'We'll buy a door mat that squeaks when you stand on it!'

Cynthia demonstrated a squeak without waiting for the doormat.

In the end a compromise was reached. Bernard filled the shop window leading on to the street with colourful eye-catching goods and fixed a large sheet of white painted hardboard behind them to obscure the interior. This prevented passers by from peering into the living room, but it added to their curiosity. Some said Bernard must have put it there to stop Cynthia staring out of the window instead of keeping her eye on the shop; others thought it might have been plaster board that had fallen from the ceiling. A travelling salesman, calling to interest Bernard in a new brand of tinned soup, said it would be a good place to advertise and asked if he could use it to exhibit a promotional poster.

'I could let you have a dozen tins a month as free samples,' he added.

Cynthia's verdict on the quality of the soup was that it would not sell, but it did, and Bernard saw that the window display could make money for him as well as the advertiser. The next salesmen to bring their wares to the *Stores* were surprised to find it was the shopkeeper who opened the sales pitch. Within a month, the back of the window was covered with slogans and cardboard cut-outs of samples which the salesmen had left behind for display in the shop.

The success of this enterprise gave Bernard another idea for advertising. This was to pay Jonathan some extra pocket-money to walk through the village with a sandwich-board, but it was vetoed by Cynthia before Jonathan got to hear of it.

Then, one evening when Bernard was browsing over some brochures and enjoying a moment of vicarious pleasure, Cynthia dropped in front of him a copy of 'The Dewpond', a parish magazine written by the local vicar. Typed and circulated monthly by one of his churchwardens it gave details of forthcoming events in the village, and news of local interest, followed by a series of pre-paid advertisements announcing services provided by local tradesmen, and second-hand goods for sale or wanted.

'Why don't we advertise in that?' said Cynthia.

Bernard was well aware that most of the villagers were already familiar with the whereabouts of the *General Stores* and doubted if such an investment would yield a significant return, but by pledging to keep stocks of the magazine in his shop for collection by customers, he got the advertisement free.

The Talbots were in the happy position of having practically no competition from other shops in the village, which were mostly selling single products. There was, for example, a bakery in a converted barn near the church where a craftsman called Gubbins, known to everyone as 'Doughie', baked mouth-watering bread and occasional cakes. That is, cakes baked for special occasions. When Bernard was a boy the smell of yeast as he passed the barn would always make him hungry, and he could remember villagers bringing their weekend joints to be roasted in the ovens after the bread had been baked. Cynthia liked old Doughie, and often walked up to the bakery to collect her bread before breakfast, but she was not yet accustomed to the local love of nicknames and it was a long time before she could bring herself to adopt the vernacular. In any case, she had been brought up to believe it wrong to be familiar with the servants. Then, one day when she was least expecting it, Doughie took her to one side and said : 'If you aren't goin' t'call me Doughie, like what others do, I 'ont bake any more o' your bloomers!'

It was the last time she called him 'Mr Baker'.

There was also a butcher's shop in the village, attached to a house called *The Brambles.* Next to it there used to be a slaughter house where sheep, pigs and bullocks were put to death with gunshot, knives and hatchets. The animals died in pools of blood before being washed down, cut up and prepared for sale in the shop. Bernard used to hear their screams as he walked past on his way to the village school but he took it all in his stride and gave little thought to what was happening. Shortly after the war, regulations were tightened up and a closure notice served on the slaughter house. Everything sold in the shop thereafter came from a properly regulated abattoir where more humane methods of killing the animals were used. The slaughter house was cleaned out and converted to a stable, and the neighbouring field became a playground for horses ridden by the butcher's daughter. Bernard never told Cynthia about this and she bought her meat in ignorance of how it was once prepared. She was also ignorant of the butcher's name. She knew him as Mr Butcher because she heard the locals calling him 'Butch'. His real name was George Trotter, but he made no attempt to correct her. He said 'Mr Butcher' gave him the dignity which his nickname lacked.

Where once there was a forge now stood a garage and filling station. Sam Burns, the old blacksmith, had trained his son to shoe horses and bend metal over the anvil, but when horses became few and motors more frequent he converted the workshop into a garage and sent his son to learn how to service a motor car. The shed in which he used to store coal and timber for the forge was cleaned up and now functioned as a shop where cigarettes, sweets and newspapers were sold. Bobby, the old blacksmith's son, worked in the garage and attended the pump, while his wife Linda looked after the shop and helped out on the pump when necessary. On Saturday mornings an itinerant barber, known only as 'Clippy', brought his equipment to the back of the shop for those who wanted a shave or a haircut.

In deference to its origins, and Sam Burns' family nickname, the entire premises were known as 'Blackie's'.

Not to be confused with young 'Clippy', a man known locally as 'Chippy' ran a fish and chip shop from a shed in his garden. He lived with his wife in an old and draughty cottage built originally for a farm labourer. Each night from Tuesday to Saturday he would stand bare-chested beside a trough of boiling oil and fry cutlets of cod, or haddock, or plaice, and bucket-loads of chipped potatoes, while his wife stood ready to scoop them onto greaseproof paper and wrap them in newspaper for their customers to take away. His equipment was crude and patently unsafe, but it had never let him down and he kept it scrupulously clean.

The shop was chiefly patronised by teenagers spending their pocket money on the opposite sex, and lonely pensioners eking out their meagre resources.

Chippy was a jovial man, in his late fifties, and his readiness to sing to customers earned him the additional sobriquet : 'Chirpy'. Bernard and Cynthia knew him as Chirpy Chippy!

There were other examples where trading was taking place in residential quarters although none of them could truly be called a shop. Molly Trumshaw, at Holly Corner, was a seamstress who used her mother's Singer sewing machine to make dresses and curtains, or repair them. Martin Cooper, a cobbler, repaired shoes in a back room of his cottage and made new pairs for those who could afford them. Charlie Harmer, a second-hand bookseller, made more money taking bets for a bookmaker than selling other people's books.

Bernard reasoned that none of the other traders would suffer if he were to increase business for the *General Stores*. Because the inhabitants of nearby towns and hamlets were becoming more mobile it was likely that some might be persuaded to visit the village of Backwater. Of those who did some might then be encouraged to spend money in his shop. Others might also buy from Doughie, once they could smell his bread; some would buy strings of Butch's prize winning sausages; and almost everyone who came by car would call for oil or petrol at Blackie's Garage. He wasn't sure about Molly or Martin, but everyone, he believed, including Charlie Harmer, would be better off. It was important, therefore, to catch the attention of travellers as soon as they entered the village, so he made two large notice boards out of a sheet of plywood on which he painted a large arrow and the words TO THE GENERAL STORES. He then took the boards to opposite ends of the village and nailed them to signposts marking the Backwater boundary.

As soon as the county highways authority heard about this they demanded their removal, but Bernard resisted. He said he had as much right to put up a direction sign as the Automobile Association, who often guided motorists in that way. He did, however, offer to pay a wayleave for as long as the boards remained where he put them. When that failed he wrote a letter to *The Scribe*, a newspaper distributed in the Backwater area, suggesting the county council's refusal to accept his money meant they were not in need of it. 'Presumably', he wrote, 'we may take it that the council will not be increasing our rates in the foreseeable future'. This provoked enough correspondence to keep the subject alive for several weeks and brought many new customers to the *General Stores*.

The Talbots' profits began to rise but Bernard was a realist and knew that what went up was likely, sooner or later, to come down. It was a view shared by Cynthia, whose pessimism predicted the downturn long before it happened. Meanwhile, Jonathan and Amy were enjoying the reputation of having illustrious parents and thought it a huge joke when their father was invited to be guest of honour at the junior school prize-giving ceremony.

'You do know what it'll mean, Dad, don't you? A stiff arm handing out books all afternoon.'

Bernard winced. He remembered when he won a school prize for coming top of the class in mental arithmetic he was awarded a book of poetry, which was not his favourite subject. Aware that he would have no say in the choice of prizes to be awarded on this occasion, he decided to add a gift to each of the winners in order to compensate them if they were given a book they did not like.

The idea was fine, but it presupposed he would know what they *would* like! He wondered what *he* would have liked as reparation for that book of poetry. In his mind's eye he saw himself as a small boy on his way home from school calling at a tuck shop on the corner of the street and buying that little red box of exotic preserves. It made his mouth water to think of it.

On the day of the prize-giving he carried with him to the ceremony a large cardboard carton which he slipped casually under his chair on the rostrum. When the moment came for him to perform his duties, he stood up and pulled the carton out from between his legs. Then, to the astonishment of the headmaster, as he handed out the awards he picked from the carton a small box of Sun Maid Raisins which he added to the book.

Next morning there were some parents who thought the gift was rather mean for a man of Bernard's standing, but the recipients themselves had nothing but praise for the gesture. In the days that followed, a steady stream of customers called at the shop for repeat prescriptions.

Bernard did not allow the honour to go to his head, but it seemed to confirm that there were many people in the village who had a high opinion of him. It was an impression that he would soon exploit to the full.

After the excitement of seeing their name in the local paper following Bernard's clash with the local council, he and his wife became regular readers of *The Scribe*. They looked forward to reading what was happening in neighbouring areas and about subjects in which they shared an interest. It came as a shock, therefore, when they read one week that an application had been made to the district planning authority by a national chain of retailers for permission to develop a site on the outskirts of Backwater as a supermarket.

Chapter 3

Bernard was convinced that once they knew a supermarket was likely to move in to the neighbourhood the residents of Backwater would rebel and rise in opposition. In this respect he shared the insularity of preachers and politicians in thinking they spoke for the majority when they mixed only, or largely, with like-minded brethren. The villagers with whom Bernard came into contact were mostly his customers and longstanding friends of his parents. They had often said how glad they were to have a shop in the village where they could still get a personal service, and he knew from his own experience, as one who had moved recently from an urban area, what a joy it was to be free of long queues and uniformed staff at multiple check-outs. Cynthia lost no opportunity to stress this point if any of her customers showed signs of impatience while she was attending to others in the shop.

Bernard knew there were some people in the village who read *The Scribe* and would have seen the item about a supermarket, but he recognised there would be others who were as yet unaware of the proposal, so he cut the paragraph out of his copy of the paper and pasted it prominently in his shop window. He also bought extra copies of the paper and took them by hand to the butcher, baker and garage proprietor. To his dismay, they were as unconcerned as if he had told them it would soon be raining. They seemed convinced that the application would be quickly rejected but Bernard assured them that an organisation rich enough to own and stock a supermarket was unlikely to lack the resources to pursue its quest for a new outlet. He said it was up to everyone in the village to do all in their power to resist the intrusion.

'What do you suggest we do, then?' asked Doughie, somewhat surprised at Bernard's rhetoric.

'Well, to start with,' said Bernard, 'we must collect signatures on a petition.'

When he put the proposal to Butch, his response was equally dismissive.

'What good'll that do?' he grumbled. 'Better we put up barriers and pelt the opposition.' Aggression was part of his nickname.

Bobby Burns' idea was at least more practical. He said he would put stickers on cars when they filled up with petrol at his garage.

Bernard went back to his shop and decided the best way to get things going was to take action himself. So he typed out the following message on the largest sheet of paper that would go through his typewriter and attached it to a clipboard with a wad of blank sheets on which he expected to secure the signatures of everyone in the village :-

We, the undersigned, being quite satisfied with the shops available to us in Backwater, object most strongly to the proposal to build a supermarket on our doorstep and urge the Council to reject the application for planning consent.

The first three customers to call at the shop next morning signed the petition, but the fourth refused. He said he agreed in principle, but didn't want to put his name down in case it got on some kind of black list. If he had seen the expression on Bernard's face he would have known he was on one such list already!

By the end of the day the ratio of those who had signed the petition to those who resisted remained at three to one. Bernard wondered what he would have to do before others recognised the danger they were facing.

'There'll be no shops left in the village before they know what's hit 'em!'

Cynthia's reaction was typically downbeat. 'P'raps we'd better sell up and move out. Once the word gets around we shan't be able to find a buyer.'

When she saw the look on Bernard's face she wished she had kept the thought to herself. After a moment's reflection, he relaxed.

'I think I'd rather stay, and let the supermarket buy us out when they discover we're hampering their business.'

They were brave words, which he barely believed, but enough to steady his wife who said she would of course stand by him even if they went under.

Meanwhile, Bobby Burns was working hard on his sticker idea. He composed a slogan and wrote it out by hand on a roll of self-adhesive labels which he peeled off and stuck to the windscreen of every car as it pulled away from the petrol pump. Because the message could only be read from the outside of the car most of the drivers were unaware of it until they next stopped and the slogan became widely distributed before any of them could dispute it. Bernard saw it several times as cars drew up at his shop, and he felt a tinge of envy that he had not thought of it himself. It was, he proclaimed, a super slogan which had the merit of saying all that was needed in a few words.

By the end of the day 'SAY NO TO A SUPERMARKET' was the subject of conversation throughout the village.

More of Bernard's customers signed the petition, but he knew there were still many who resisted. He had clearly been wrong to assume everyone in the village shared his opinion about the undesirability of having a supermarket on their doorstep. He resolved to explain to one and all why they should oppose the project. Yet, the more he thought about it the harder it was to express his conviction convincingly. To say bluntly that a supermarket would put him out of business would sound selfish, but that was the nub of the issue. To get others to support him he would have to convey the extent to which they also would suffer once his shop was forced to close, and to convince them that other shops in the village would inevitably follow suit. The people who would be hardest hit would be those without transport who were unable to do their shopping outside the village, and there were many who would miss the convenience of slipping into his local store for a last minute purchase or previously forgotten item. The problem was, how to get the message across?

It was not an argument that Bernard could put in a few words to stick on motor cars, or even in his window, so he persuaded the chairman of the parish council to convene a meeting and get the matter discussed publicly.

Parish meetings were normally held only once a year, but the chairman agreed to call an Extraordinary Meeting.

The village hall was a popular venue for whist drives, barn dances and wedding receptions, but parish meetings were normally less well attended. On this occasion the use of the word extraordinary created considerable interest and with fifteen minutes to go before the meeting was due to start the hall was already full. Extra benches had to be rushed over from the nearby school and once they were occupied people were left to lean against the walls and wish they had come earlier. Debate began long before the meeting officially opened, for many people held strong views on the subject and were keen to rehearse their opinions with anyone in earshot. The noise level rose as arguments began but dropped abruptly when the parish chairman entered. Accompanied by his lady clerk he walked swiftly down the hall and took his seat at the baize-covered table facing the audience. It surprised him to find so many people waiting for him.

The chairman, Mr Archibald Thurrock, was a retired solicitor who had lived in Backwater all his life. Short of stature but not of words, he had a reputation for pomposity but was respected in the village as one of their Elders. Rumour had it that he owed his election as chairman to the fact that he owned one of the few large houses with a garden big enough to hold the annual summer fete.

The hubbub in the hall resumed but was not allowed to continue. Mr Thurrock tapped the table with his gavel and declared the meeting open.

'I expect you all know why we are here,' he began, 'or so many of you wouldn't have come. We face the prospect of having a supermarket operating in the area and opinions are mixed as to whether this will be a good thing or bad. Some see it as inevitable, a sign of the times; others as a threat to our rural way of living. I am going to call upon Mr Bernard Talbot to open the discussion.'

Bernard stood up, but the chairman had not yet finished his introduction.

'Mr Talbot, as many of you know, is the owner of our long-established *General Stores* which has been in his family for generations. He is particularly well qualified to talk to us on this subject because, although he was born and bred in Backwater, he experienced some of the trappings of an urban environment before he came back to take over the family business.'

Bernard sensed there was a danger the chairman might go on. Already on his feet, and embarrassed by the formal introduction, he began the speech he had prepared by confessing he felt like a batsman standing at the wicket waiting to face a succession of unknown bowlers.

'How's that!' shouted a wag from the back of the hall.

Bernard treated the quip as a question. 'Because I know some of you don't share my view about the coming of a supermarket.'

Mr Thurrock feared Bernard had taken his eye off the ball and resumed the role of chairman. 'Mr Talbot is going to spell out his reasons for telling us why we should 'say no to a supermarket?'

Bernard resented the prompting, but accepted the cue. 'In the first place,' he said, 'there won't be room for them and us. By which I mean, if you let in a supermarket you'll effectively be kicking out your local tradesmen.'

'Oh, so we're playing football now, are we?' cried the wag.

'No, we're not playing games at all,' said Bernard, 'it's much too serious for that. If it were a game there'd be rules for fair play, and anyone could win, but what I'm talking about is no contest. Once a supermarket gets in, there'll be no chance for any of us to survive.'

'What about us customers?' shouted someone from the floor.

'It's you I'm thinking about,' said Bernard, trying to recover his ground. 'You'd soon have no choice about where to do your shopping. There'd be no handy place to buy something you needed urgently, or had forgotten. And you'd find you had to buy whatever brand the supermarket stocked, which might not be the one you wanted.'

A lady in the audience took up the argument.

'There's actually more to choose from in a supermarket. And you can reach for the goods yourself. I hate asking you or Mrs Talbot to put something back on the shelf if I see something else I like the look of better.'

'Just like my missus,' came a deep voice from the crowd. 'Always changing her mind!'

'I bet she wishes she could change her old man!' came the higher pitched retort.

Several speakers then made the point that most goods cost less in a supermarket where they sell more and can buy in bulk.

Bernard's heart was sinking, for no-one yet had stood up to support him. He looked around and could see there were many in the audience who had never been to his shop. Some were young enough to be the sons or daughters of villagers he knew, but others were middle aged or elderly and might only recently have come into the village. He asked the chairman's permission to speak again.

'If you've anything new to say,' said Mr Thurrock, 'let's hear it.'

Bernard was angry 'Some people here today will find it difficult to do their shopping outside the village, because we've no longer got a bus service, and even if there were buses, who would want to carry loads of shopping home on a bus every week? I cannot believe,' he added, ' that anyone here who enjoys the country life would want to see us having to live like they do in the cities, dependent on cars, and queues, and easy credit... ' Bernard drew a deep breath and was lost for words.

Not wishing to prolong the meeting, the chairman said he thought there had been a good discussion and to Bernard's horror said it sounded to him as though the general view was that a supermarket in the district mightn't be a bad thing.

'No!' came a shout from one of the elderly ladies who, like the chairman, had lived in the village all her life. 'I say it would be a very *bad* thing. We've managed all right all these years with our own *Stores* and a butcher and baker and we don't need rows and rows of shelves packed with different varieties of the same thing.   All that's a trick to make you buy more than what you set out to buy. You might save a penny or two on some things, but you'll end up spending pounds more by the time you get out of the place.'

Bernard felt better after that and better still when the chairman asked him if he had anything further to say. Seeing that people were beginning to leave, Bernard said only that those who didn't want a supermarket in the vicinity should sign the petition in his shop. That is, if they hadn't done so already. The chairman then brought the meeting to a close, and conveniently forgot to take a vote on the outcome.

Some of the older folk stood around and offered Bernard suggestions of what they thought could be done to preserve the amenities they valued most. He made a note of what he thought would be useful but wished there had been more open support for the campaign he was trying to launch.

On his way out Mr Thurrock shook him by the hand and offered to help in any way that would be of benefit to the community. Bernard wondered if he had listened to anything he had said that evening. Then, as an afterthought, the chairman added: 'I won't say no to your campaign, but I may have to be discreet. After all, I'm supposed to be impartial in these matters. I'm sure you understand!'

When he got home that night Bernard was disappointed at the general lack of enthusiasm he had aroused and asked himself if he should go on with the campaign. It seemed that many of the residents were happy to let a supermarket in. Perhaps it was too strong to say they were happy about it, but merely being complacent would have the same result: there would be no *General Stores* and no butcher or baker left in the village. He decided he had no alternative but to go on fighting!

One of the suggestions made to him after the meeting was that they should parade through the village carrying banners explaining why they needed to oppose the project. Bernard thought this was a good idea but doubted if he would get many volunteers to carry the banners. Judging by those who spoke at the meeting in support of his proposition, few of them looked fit enough to walk around the village with an umbrella, far less a banner; and as for those who spoke against him it seemed unlikely many converts would be made *en route*. In the event, with help from their mothers, he managed to recruit six young school-leavers fresh from the sixth form, who saw it as a means of having fun rather than a serious public-spirited mission.

Their first task was to construct banners. Unfortunately they made the mistake of making the banners larger and heavier than when they were boy scouts. It was a mistake they were soon to regret. Wisely they left it to Bernard to compose the slogans, which included such gems as the following:-

Buy at a supermarket then bye-bye to your shops.

Say no now as later may be too late.

Save pennies now but lose local shops forever.

Support your local shops and shop the developers.

'Excuse me, Mr Talbot,' said Mathew when shown the slogans. 'Shouldn't that be – and *stop* the developers?'

'No,' said Bernard, 'that's Trade Union language. People will understand.'

18

At last, when the words had been painted on strips of canvas and the canvas fastened to poles for carrying aloft, the lads set off to scenes of merriment and boisterous behaviour. All that was missing was any obvious commitment to the cause.

The reaction of most villagers was non-committal, but some raised a cheer or two and others shouted abuse. The density of dwellings being decidedly low, the boys had considerable distances to trudge between houses and many of the banners were drooping by the time they reached the end of their journey. Bernard was pleased with their effort but had no means of knowing if it would result in any more tangible support for his campaign. He gave each boy a box of chocolate candies and persuaded them to hold on to the banners for use on another occasion.

The following week a few more signatures were added to the petition, but the total gathered was less than Bernard had anticipated and fewer than was likely to influence the planners in reaching their decision. Time was getting short. Bernard knew that objections to the application had to be made before the next meeting of the planning committee. He must, therefore, think of other ways to alert inhabitants to the fate he was predicting.

The word fate reminded him of an event which was due to take place in Mr Thurrock's garden in two weeks' time.

'Everyone will be going to the village fete,' he told Cynthia, 'so that's where we must make our last stand.'

It was an unintended pun, but the idea was forming in his mind of setting out a stall where people could be shown why it was important for their future not to have a supermarket on their doorstep, and where they could sign the petition to register their opposition. He made his ideas known to Mr Thurrock, and got a guarded response.

'I don't mind a bit of propaganda,' he said 'so long as there's no strong-arm stuff from the likes of your Banner Boys!'

Bernard was surprised to know that the parish chairman had been aware of the recent parade, but assured him the boys would be under his control and well behaved. It was a rash boast, but one he felt confident in making - with the help, perhaps, of a few more candies. He had been wrong about the number of villagers who would support his campaign, and he would soon be wrong again about the efficacy of candies to quell the exuberance of youth.

Chapter 4

Bernard's Banner Boys, as they were now known, welcomed the prospect of playing a part in the village fete instead of just drifting from one stall to another as they had done in previous years. They were not at all intimidated by Bernard's strictures on their behaviour. After warning them not to cause offence he instructed them to make sure that everyone at the fete would be able to see the banners and read what was written on them. As an afterthought, he added: 'If you can think of other ways to put across the message, feel free to do so.'

Anyone who has ever taken part in preparing for a fete, wherever it is held and for whatever good cause, will know how much work has to be done on the night before, and how dependent the organisers are on a number of loyal and reliable supporters. Bernard had not previously been among the helpers at Backwater, although he had given a hand at school fetes when his children first went to school. He was greeted at *The Willows* by Mr Thurrock who introduced him to the regular supporters as they arrived to prepare the garden for the following day's invasion. Most of the regulars knew Bernard very well and were pleased to have him with them as another helper. They showed him where to find the posts and trestle tables and how best to put them up. Mr Barlow, the organiser, who lived next door to *The Willows*, gave them all instructions about where on the lawn their stalls were to be positioned.

The fun of hammering in posts and tying ropes to tarpaulin covers in case it should rain was part of the enjoyment of such occasions and Bernard entered into the spirit wholeheartedly. It was while he was sharing jokes with his neighbours that six youths arrived on the scene with their slogan-bearing banners. Without waiting for directions they began to drive their poles into the ground alongside six of the stalls that had just been erected. The mood of Bernard's neighbours changed abruptly. They had recognised the boys from their recent tour of the village and regarded their action as belligerent. The organiser was sent for and he urged Bernard to call off his Banner Boys before they disrupted the proceedings.

'Can't you tell them to fix their banners somewhere else?' said Mr Barlow, not wishing to quarrel with his latest recruit.

'I daresay they've only put 'em there temporarily,' Bernard pleaded.

'They'll carry them round tomorrow when the fete begins.'

Hearing this, one of the boys whispered in Bernard's ear that they had fixed the banners to the ground so they would have their hands free to attend to some other ideas they'd been working on. With no time to query the nature of their ideas, Bernard asked them politely to pick up the banners and put them somewhere else. Reluctantly they responded, offering mild apologies as they pulled the poles from under the feet of six aggrieved stall holders. Sloping off with banners under their arms they struck them into the ground on either side of the driveway and saw, as they passed through the gate, a hugely superior banner had been thrown across the entrance. Roped to the trees on either side of the path, it announced, as it had done for many years on these occasions: -

WELCOME TO YOUR VILLAGE FETE.

The day of the fete opened with blue skies and no clouds. The air was warm and the breeze gentle. Villagers took their lunch early and set off for *The Willows* in time for the gates to open at 2.15. First to arrive was Vernon Lovelock, the vicar, and he waited at the gate as he did at church on Sundays so that he could chat with his parishioners. His first victim was Mrs Ravenscourt whose main interest in the fete was buying home baked produce from stalls around the perimeter. The moment the Reverend Lovelock caught her eye he directed it upwards towards the message over the entrance. Mrs Ravenscourt had the impression he wanted her to believe he was communing with the deity.

'Do you see what I see?' he asked her.

Probably not, thought Mrs Ravenscourt, who was less devout than she pretended. However, not wishing to offend him, she looked up and smiled courteously.

'If you mean a clear blue sky, I certainly do. Isn't it wonderful how the weather is always fine for the fete? I expect you put in a good word for us!'

Mrs Ravenscourt did not wait for a response but hurried into the garden to be sure of getting the best of the cakes before they were taken.

Most of his parishioners were familiar with the vicar's habit of throwing his eyes skywards, so when he greeted the Marshall family as they approached the entrance they did not bother to look up.

'We've been here before, Vicar, so we know the way in.'

The Revd Lovelock was lost for words, and the Marshalls passed into the garden without looking back. His spirits rose, however, when he saw that the next arrivals were long-standing members of his congregation and regular supporters of the annual fete.

'Good afternoon, my friends,' he chanted. 'Or, as it says up there, welcome!'

Albert and Peggy Thrower followed his eyes to the banner, but saw nothing odd about it and walked on.

It was not until Mr Formby, the schoolmaster, saw it that any comment was made about the spelling, for it now said:

WELCOME TO THE VILLAGE FATE.

'I hope none of my kids sees that,' he muttered. 'Their spelling is bad enough without that sort of encouragement.'

Saddened by the episode, the vicar decided it was time for him to go in. On his way he met Mr Barlow coming in the opposite direction.

'Did you see my banner over the gate?' asked organiser, uncomfortably out of breath. He had just been alerted by the schoolmaster to what he called 'an unscholarly introduction'.

'I did indeed!' said the vicar. 'It looks splendid!' He made no further comment lest it was Mr Barlow who had made the spelling mistake.

Mr Barlow was now in the awkward position of not knowing if the vicar was unable to spell, or if he had misunderstood the schoolmaster and there was some other blemish on the banner.

They both decided it was better to change the subject, and walked on together into the garden. On each side of the driveway, as they walked, they passed slogans attached to poles placed there the night before by Bernard's youthful supporters. At the edge of the lawn they encountered a boy on stilts who offered to teach them how to walk-on-high for ten pence a go.

'All proceeds go to the church,' said Lenny, as he balanced effortlessly on his wooden legs.

Mr Barlow recognised the youth as one of Bernard's Banner Boys.

'All right,' said Mr Barlow, surprisingly calm. 'I'll let you teach me if you'll take me back to the entrance so I can look closer at the welcome sign.'

Lenny panicked and fell off his stilts.

'Sorry, Guv,' he said, picking himself up and staring at the grass. 'I've just busted my crutch!'

The organiser was now pretty sure he knew who had tampered with his banner, and raced off in search of Bernard. The vicar feared that at any

23

moment he might be invited to contribute his ten pennyworth, so he scurried across the lawn with as much speed in one direction as Mr Barlow was making in the other. The boys laughed as they watched him bestowing blessings on members of his congregation, and nodding silently to those who never went to church.

After such a hasty retreat the vicar was relieved to come across a stall run by the charming Chatham sisters, Angela and Mavis.

'Ah, I see you are selling **Home Made Cakes**. How very generous of you. Now let me see; what are my favourites?'

The sisters blushed and glanced at each other to see who would tell him the truth.

'Vicar, we have a confession to make. All the cakes you can see today were bought from the bakery.'

'Never mind,' said the vicar, in his most ecclesiastical manner. 'I shall eat them as though you had made them yourselves.'

Leaving the two ladies to wonder if he really meant it, he thrust a currant bun into his cassock and continued his tour of the stalls.

Bob and Vera Bagley were in charge of the **Tombola** stall where a variety of pots, packets and bottles were laid out on a table with numbers attached.

'Good afternoon, Vicar,' said Mrs Bagley. 'Can we persuade you to buy a ticket? If anything on the table has a number round its collar that matches the number on your ticket you win it.'

Vernon was never more conscious of the collar he was wearing.

'I'm afraid I must pass. You know, it's not in my province to gamble!'

Bob Bagley had no such inhibition and was quick to respond.

'I'll bet you bless our takings on Sunday!'

Vera was embarrassed and tried to soothe his feelings, but the vicar smiled and walked on. At the **Coconut Shy** he was reminded of collars again. All the coconuts seemed to be wearing them, and they all had a word written on them! On closer inspection he saw that each of the targets to be shied at carried the word 'supermarket'. Why, he wondered, did someone not remove the labels showing where they were bought?

Mr Barlow had by now caught up with Bernard. Thinking he was coming to sign the petition, Bernard held out a pen, but it was waved aside.

'Those boys of yours have tampered with my banner.'

'Oh, surely not,' said Bernard, 'they've made plenty of their own.'

It was hard for Mr Barlow to believe that Bernard knew nothing about the change of spelling on his notice over the entrance, but when he realised this was a prank which the boys had thought up by themselves he conceded it was a clever stunt.

Bernard was glad to be released from blame.

'Can't say as I'd welcome our fate if we do get a supermarket,' he said, looking for support. 'Would you?'

Mr Barlow was not to be drawn, but he did show that he was no mean player with words.

'You can tell those lads of yours that I don't approve, but I do admit that reaching the banner was a remarkable feat.'

Back to the vicar. He had now reached a stall which he could not remember seeing in previous years. Resting on a trestle table, an air gun was pointing at cut-outs of people in various poses: standing, sitting, lying down and running. Slung above the figures was a title board saying this was a **Miniature Shooting Range**. A notice on the table said ten points would be scored for hitting where it would kill, five for where it would wound and none if the shot landed anywhere else. Vernon was aghast. Indignantly, he remonstrated with the stall holder that this was a totally evil and unchristian pursuit, but Ted Buckley would have none of that. He was an old soldier who reminded the vicar he had fought, like many others, in the name of christianity and would probably be dead now if he hadn't known how to use a gun.

'But we are now at peace,' protested Vernon.

'So was I when I were your age!' came the reply.

The vicar was in such a hurry to move on, that he did not see another notice which Bernard's boys had hung from the table, below the rifle. This one said: BACKWATER NEEDS A SUPERMARKET LIKE A HOLE IN THE HEAD.

The Banner Boys by this time had set their sights on the **Lucky Dip** which was being run by a very pretty teenager called Dolly Peacock. On the floor was a large box filled with sawdust in which had been concealed a number of small packages. Some of the packets contained a gift, but others were empty. It was part of the fun to discover whether your dip produced a gift or a blank.

Banner Boy Billy had brought along another box which he wanted to substitute for the one which Dolly was looking after. He and his friends had worked out a plan for doing this. The plan was that while Billy was chatting with Dolly, another of the Banner Boys would happen to pass and Billy would invite him to join them. When a suitable opportunity arose the other Banner Boy, namely Freddie, would offer to look after the stall while Billy took Dolly for a walk round the garden. Dolly was known to fancy Billy and she would understand this to be a euphemism for a snog behind the potting shed. As soon as they were out of sight, Freddie would swop over the boxes and thereafter the packages lifted from the lucky dip would contain either a voucher for products from the *General Stores* or blanks in the form of slogans saying

STOP THE SUPERMARKET. By the time Dolly discovered the switch, Billy and Freddie would be busy in a far corner of the garden organising another event.

The four Banner Boys who were given no part to play in this exercise said it would fail, but it didn't. The only thing that did not work out according to plan was that Billy and Dolly did not return from the potting shed and Freddie was left to look after the Dip for the rest of the afternoon.

When the Reverend Lovelock found Mr Barlow he complained about the inclusion in the fete of a stall encouraging 'the killing instinct'. Mr Barlow assured him it was only a game and no worse than those he would find nowadays on videos and computers.

'But I don't have a computer,' said the vicar.

Mr Barlow was trying to think of an alternative justification when the vicar made what sounded like an unexpected retraction.

'I suppose it wouldn't be so bad,' he said, 'if they changed the scoring system so that a hit where it *didn't* hurt would get 10 points, and a wound of any kind would disqualify.'

A popular feature at all fetes, is the **Balloon Race**, which is not really a race at all but a contest to reward the sender of a balloon which travels the farthest.

The garden at *The Willows* was surrounded by trees but large enough to allow balloons to escape into the sky when despatched from the centre of the lawn on a calm day. The weather forecast that morning was for a clear sky and light wind, so Mr Barlow set up a cylinder of hydrogen gas where a balloon could be launched with every expectation of it travelling into the distance without colliding with a conifer.

Banner Boys Mathew and Gerald joined the queue early enough to help Mr Johnson put the names and addresses of contestants on a tag and attach it to a balloon prior to take off. While that was happening Tommy was busy stamping slogans on a box of unfilled balloons. It was Tommy who thought of the idea. He had once been given a printing set for his birthday and there were just enough letters in it to make up the words NO SUPERMARKET. By inking the letters and pressing them on the rubber surface of an unfilled balloon they produced an image which grew in size as the balloon inflated. Mr Johnson was so intent on making sure the balloons he was filling did not fly off the hydrogen cylinder prematurely that he failed to notice the message they were carrying.

One of them landed eight miles away, near where it was planned to build the supermarket. The site had not yet been cleared for development and it was overgrown with gorse and bramble, so the balloon burst on landing and its message was never read by those it was meant to influence. Those which fell short in the parish chairman's garden, however, were being read by everyone present at the fete.

The recent parish meeting had already shown that not everyone in the village shared Bernard's objection to a supermarket and among those at the fete that afternoon was a group of youths who came specifically to disrupt his campaign. They watched the Banner Boys distributing their slogans and then went round the garden systematically removing them, or reversing their message.

It was late in the afternoon when Bernard left his stall and set off on a tour of inspection to see what was happening elsewhere in the garden. Instead of finding banners and placards carrying the slogans he had composed for the occasion he came across several that urged readers to SAY NOW TO A SUPERMARKET. Angry at what he thought was a careless slip of typography, he raced off in search of 'his boys', only to find them coming away from the shooting range carrying a length of rope. Bernard was not a violent man but the temptation to take the rope and wrap it round their necks was overwhelming. However, there was a look of innocence on their faces which calmed his temper, until he caught sight of the placard hanging from the table saying simply : BACKWATER NEEDS A SUPERMARKET. There was no reference to a hole in the head! His anger returned, but this time it was met by laughter from another group of boys, who were watching him from behind the stall. Bernard guessed they were the ones who had interfered with the slogan but before he could check this out he recognised his own boys running at them and saw them all disappear together into a cluster of rhododendron bushes.

Some minutes later Bernard saw the boys running towards the centre of the lawn where balloons were still being released. Tommy, who was carrying the rope, placed it on the ground beside the hydrogen cylinder and called upon his friends to round up their supporters for a **Tug-of-War**. Without hesitation they deserted the balloon race, and got Freddie to abandon the lucky dip. They then went in search of Billy, who reluctantly returned from a summer house at the bottom of the garden, leaving Dolly to find her own way back to the stall she had deserted.

Those against a supermarket were urged to fall in behind the only banner left saying NO TO A SUPERMARKET, while those of the opposite persuasion were steered towards the mutilated placard from the shooting range saying BACKWATER NEEDS A SUPERMARKET. When each side had filled its quota of rope they braced themselves for battle.

All they needed now was a neutral umpire. By common consent Mr Thurrock was sent for and, after a few words of explanation, he agreed to adjudicate on condition that no-one dug their toes in to his lawn or pulled the other side over onto a flower bed.

The word spread rapidly and most of the visitors, together with many of the stall holders, formed a circle round the lawn to watch the event. Mr Thurrock borrowed a gun from the shooting range and fired it into the air to start the contest.

Bernard foresaw the outcome before the shot was fired. Not only were the Banner Boys younger and thinner than their opponents but they were mostly supported by frail and elderly men, whereas their rivals were in the company of overweight and middle-aged newcomers to the village. There was a lot of cheering and dogs barked, while the contestants sweated and swore, until the heavier side gained momentum and pulled the other side over.

Bernard had watched from among the crowd and as his supporters fell he felt his campaign went over with them. He walked back to his stall and stared sadly at the small number of signatures which had been added to his petition that afternoon. His daughter Amy, who arrived in time to see the result of the tug-of-war, put out her arm to comfort him.

'Never mind, Dad,' she said, 'I'll ride through the village like Lady Godiva and see if that gets the message across!'

Chapter 5

There were two surprises for Bernard in the week following the fete. The first was when he discovered Amy was taking riding lessons from the butcher's daughter, Daphne, and was seriously intending to ride bare-breasted through the streets of Backwater. Bernard had said nothing to his wife about Amy's remark at the fete because he thought she was joking, so when Cynthia was asked by a customer if it was true that her daughter was taking riding lessons she was taken by surprise. The shock was compounded when her informant added that he supposed she was planning to drive her father on his delivery rounds in a pony trap.

Bernard was confronted by an angry wife when he got back to the shop that evening.

'Did you know Amy was taking riding lessons?'

'Well, yes, but I didn't think she was serious about it.'

'And did you intend buying a trap so she could help you with the deliveries?'

This was an unexpected twist. The idea had never occurred to him but before he could deny it Cynthia's expression had changed.

'Perhaps you do need some help now that deliveries are getting heavier. Why don't you sell the tricycle,' she said, 'and buy a van?'

Bernard gasped, and Cynthia mistook his silence for embarrassment at being found out.

'Did Amy hear you talking about a pony and trap,' she continued, 'and is that why she has taken an interest in horses?'

'No,' said Bernard, 'I've never even thought about a pony and trap, but I think I know what she's up to.' He then told Cynthia what Amy had said to him at the fete and confessed he feared she was planning an early morning parade through the village.

Cynthia was horrified. The thought of having a streaker in the village was bad enough, but to have one in the family! Besides, it would be bad for business!

'You're not going to let her do it, are you?' she pleaded.

Had Bernard been able to read Cynthia's thoughts he might have argued that it would be *good* for business, but he asked her how she expected him to stop the girl.

'We can't chain her to the bed!' he protested.

'Then we must tell Mr Butcher to chain up the horses.' In her distress, Cynthia reverted to using the name by which she had always known George Trotter.

'I'll have another word with George,' said Bernard.

When he mentioned it to the butcher, George laughed.

'Your Amy may be brave enough to expose her bosom, but our Daphne's daft enough to ride that horse o' hers with a bare bottom!'

'Well, I hope she doesn't,' said Bernard. 'It might convey entirely the wrong message.'

'What, then, do you reckon she wants to tell us?' asked the butcher.

'Amy says she wants to do for the village what Lady Godiva did for Coventry.'

'There weren't any supermarkets about in her day, though, were there?'

Bernard decided it was better not to pursue the matter.

Bernard's second surprise came the next day when Charlie Plumstead, the dairyman, walked into the shop and brought him news that plans to build a supermarket on the edge of the village had been rejected by the council. Bernard wanted to throw his hands in the air, or somersault across the counter, like they do at football matches when a goal is scored.

'Looks like our campaign succeeded,' said Charlie, who had been a signatory to the petition. 'I suppose we can celebrate a victory!'

Bernard looked for something suitable to offer this bringer of glad tidings, but all he could find was a bottle of Babycham.

'This'll have to do, I'm afraid,' he said, 'but it's the nearest I can get to the real thing on the spur of the moment.'

Cynthia came in from the living room to find them drinking from a couple of plastic mugs, and empty bottles of Babycham lying on the counter.

'What was that in aid of?' she asked when Charlie had gone.

Bernard told her the good news, but couldn't satisfy her curiosity about where Charlie Plumstead got the information.

'Don't you think we ought to check up on the story in case it's only a rumour?'

'Sweetheart!' said Bernard, impatiently, 'you know how much I value your opinion, but couldn't you, just this once, accept some good news without blowing cold air on it!'

She picked up the empty bottles and plastic cups from the counter and walked back into the living room.

Later that morning Bernard decided perhaps he had better seek confirmation from the council and telephoned their offices. 'Yes,' they said, 'it was true that the developer's application had not been accepted in its present form because the site on which they proposed to build was too close to a school and a churchyard. Also, the design they submitted did not blend with other properties in the neighbourhood.'

'Thank goodness for that,' said Bernard, unable to conceal his excitement. 'We don't want a supermarket on our doorstep, do we?'

'They will, of course, be able to re-submit,' said the council officer, 'if they can modify or redesign their plans to meet our requirements.'

Bernard put down the telephone and swore.

So, the battle was not yet won! There was still time to rally opposition, and perhaps persuade the planners to refuse permission a second time. Or, the developers might back off in favour of another site. In either case, Bernard resolved to take advantage of the opportunity to make hay while the sun was shining.

With this thought in mind he returned to Cynthia and confessed that he had been unwise to treat second-hand news as unquestionably reliable. He told her what he had learned from the council and said they must prepare for a long struggle. Cynthia had no wish to spoil the enjoyment of such a rare apology and when he began to talk about redecorating the premises she made no attempt to dampen his enthusiasm.

They had done a certain amount of decorating themselves at the bungalow but it was not their favourite occupation.

Bernard's concept of redecorating was to brush a coat of emulsion over the walls and non-drip paint on the doors and window frames. Cynthia, however, insisted on a thorough wash-down and two coats of emulsion on the walls, and an undercoat followed by gloss on the woodwork.

'Will we have time to do all that?'

'We must do it properly, like the professionals,' said Cynthia.

'Then let's employ the professionals.'

'They'd want us to shut the shop for a week.'

'Wouldn't we have to do that anyway?'

'Not if we work 'after hours'.'

Bernard thought they did that already, but said nothing.

Cynthia pursued her line of thinking.

'I don't mind shutting shop at 5 o'clock,' she said, 'if we give fair notice, but I wouldn't like to shut our customers out altogether for a week.'

'Mind you,' said Bernard, ready to concede the argument, 'when you think about it, there's nowhere else for them to go, is there?'

'That's the whole point,' said Cynthia. 'There *will* be once there's a supermarket; so we'd better not upset them now.'

Bernard agreed, and prepared for the task.

All DIY experts know the value of time spent on preparation. Bernard and Cynthia were no experts but they knew that meant more than just assembling a sheet of sandpaper and a paint brush. They discussed the options and decided what needed to be replaced, repaired or repositioned, and how to create the effect they wanted. To be more precise, it was Cynthia who made the decisions, and Bernard who decided to go along with her suggestions.

A notice was placed on the shop door advising customers to expect some dislocation for a few days, and then began the weary business of clearing the decks for action. Goods had to be moved and stacked elsewhere; shelves dismantled; and surfaces covered with dust sheets.

For a day or two there was little to show for their efforts. Walls were washed and rubbed down, brackets removed and cracks filled, until the place looked uninhabited, but once the paint began to go on there were daily signs of progress.

Bernard would have liked to announce that the shop would open later in the morning and close earlier at night, but Cynthia reminded him how important it was to inconvenience their customers as little as possible.

'I suppose it doesn't matter if we inconvenience ourselves!'

'It was your idea to decorate, and yours to come here in the first place.' As usual, Cynthia had the last word.

So Bernard got up early in order to remove the dust sheets and re-stack those goods he thought might be wanted during the day. Most people in the village were considerate and chose alternative items when their preferred goods were not accessible, but there was always the odd customer who asked for an item that was out of sight because it had not been sold recently. Cynthia would turn the place upside down to find it. Bernard would say it was out of stock.

When the painting was finished, there was still the floor to re-surface and some new light fittings to install. These were jobs they admitted they could not do themselves, so Bernard found a builder's labourer in the village who was known to earn extra money by moonlighting. He was engaged to lay rust coloured quarry tiles over the shop floor, and Bernard got his friend, Bobbie Burns, at Blackie's Garage, to fix some fluorescent tubes to the ceiling.

'Are you sure it's strip lighting you want?' queried Bobby, 'because you may need sunglasses if you do'

'Cynthia says she wants to freshen up the shop.'

Bobby pulled a face.

'A strip will make her look ghostly!'

Bernard thought he said 'ghastly' and wondered what the lad was thinking.

'On the bright side, of course,' said Bobby, unaware of Bernard's reaction, and oblivious to the pun, 'the tubes will last longer than tungsten light bulbs. And they produce more light with less electricity'.

'The alchemists' dream!' said Bernard. 'I'll settle for that.'

The day came when all the covers were removed, shelves were put back and goods re-stacked. Cynthia wore a new dress and Bernard sported the latest fashion in neck ties. A mat said WELCOME as you walked through the door and a battery-operated bell rang when the mat was stepped upon. The colour scheme was bright and unfamiliar, and customers gasped when they entered the shop. Some thought it was under new management again, and others supposed the Talbots had come into money.

'Reckon you've bin makin' too much profit!' said one of their regulars with a grin that suggested he didn't resent it.

'Do I ha' to tak' me shoes orf now afore I cum in?' asked another.

'They'll be sellin' up shortly,' confided a local gossip to his neighbour. 'You mark my words. That's a sure sign when they start smartenin' the place up!'

Bernard had more than once secretly considered selling up, but he knew he could never do that while his parents were alive, and supposed he would find it even more difficult when they were dead. Even before he embarked upon the decorating he had begun to question the wisdom of adopting shopkeeping as a career. The long-established practice of serving customers who called at the shop after it closed was a burden he had not anticipated, and there were other jobs too, that could only be done outside normal working hours so, by the time the decorating was finished, he was exhausted and desperately tired. Cynthia could see this and feared he was on the verge of a breakdown. She told him he was unfit to make his delivery round and insisted she should do it for him.

After a few rounds on the tricycle she became more determined than ever that he should buy a van.

Bernard, however, had no wish to exchange the feel of fresh air on his face for the confined space of a motorised cabin. He would miss the pleasure of pedalling his three-wheeler along the country lanes.

'There are things we need more urgently than a van,' he protested.

'Like what?' she asked, wearily.

Bernard's patience snapped. 'Like a new weighing machine with springs and a flat platform instead of the blasted pans and brass weights we've been working with. Also, it's time we got a proper till that opens and shuts at the touch of a button and has a tally roll to register the cash we're taking. One day,' he said, 'the tax man is going to insist upon it!'

'Well, if we're going to go on a spending spree,' said Cynthia, 'I'd like a new apron and some warmer shoes to wear in the shop.'

'If we had a refrigerator we wouldn't need a cold shop to keep food from going bad.'

'Where on earth would we put a refrigerator? There isn't enough room in the shop to put another box of matches!'

'We could make room for it under the counter.'

'Oh, no we can't. I'm not serving anything from under the counter. There was enough of that when the war was on!'

Bernard glimpsed a sign of contrition in Cynthia's eyes, and relaxed. The subject had changed and the threat of a motor vehicle receded.

'I suppose,' said, Cynthia, 'on second thoughts, a fridge *would* be useful. We could sell ice-creams to the tourists you keep telling me will soon be coming to the village.'

They were able at last to laugh and began to make a list of what else was needed in the shop to enhance its new image.

'We could stop using old newspapers for wrapping up the goods.'

'OK,' said Bernard. 'Let's order some carrier bags with *General Stores, Backwater* printed on them.'

Cynthia grinned. 'But what shall we do with all the old newspapers?'

'Same as we did with the humbugs,' said Bernard. 'Throw them out.'

This was the turning point when they finally gave up attempts to go on running the *Stores* as it had been run for generations. From now on they would fill the shop with goods that customers wanted to buy; not what salesmen wanted them to stock. They knew there were people in Backwater who were more fortunate than their parents had been, who had more money at their disposal, and were looking for new products to spend it on. If those people could not find what they wanted in the village they would take their custom elsewhere. That meant, if the authorities were so short-sighted as to allow it, to a supermarket.

At all costs, the Talbots were determined to keep up with the times, but to keep out the supermarket.

Chapter 6

There is nothing like a spring-clean for improving morale around the house, and the same goes for a shop. The new décor in the *General Stores* created a cheerful atmosphere and diverted conversation from the disagreeable topics of the day. Villagers vied with each other to describe their own home improvements and compared notes on costs and the choice of colours.

Because they had repositioned some of the shelves Cynthia and Bernard were constantly pulling down tins of cat food where soups had previously been kept, and packets of washing powders where once there had been breakfast cereals. They had re-arranged the shelves at various levels to accommodate more economically the packets, bottles and tins of different sizes. The space thus saved made room for some new products, like fancy biscuits and jams with exotic flavours, which had not previously been sold in the shop. To encourage sales, Bernard introduced his newly printed carrier bag, which he gave freely, and soon discovered it being used for many purposes not originally intended.

Customers also had to adapt to the changes confronting them as they entered the shop. Those with young children had to restrain them from playing with the bell on the counter or from jumping up and down on the mat as they walked in. Even the unaccompanied were unaccustomed to having their entry so conspicuously announced, and one elderly lady left immediately because it sounded like a fire alarm.

Cynthia eventually persuaded Bernard to buy a small van for local deliveries, and this soon became a familiar sight in the village, its side panels painted with the words :- *General Stores of Backwater, proprietors Bernard and Cynthia Talbot.* The tricycle was polished up and fixed to the front of the shop as a merchandising icon. (A male figure dressed in a striped apron had stood beside the butcher's shop for years.)

Inside their shop, next to the door so that no-one would miss seeing it, the

Talbots placed a refrigerator, rented from an ice cream manufacturer, which Cynthia said would serve as a receptacle for dairy produce, as well as ice creams.

Bernard's inspiration was a christmas savings scheme, designed exclusively for the accumulation of funds to be spent in the *General Stores*. By aggregating the small amounts of cash that were collected each week, and investing them prudently, he was able to distribute a larger sum at christmas than his customers would have spent had they deposited their money separately.

It was while the Talbots were preparing to stock up for when the fund was discharged that a tragedy occurred in the cottage next door which was to have the most profound consequences. As they were closing the shop, after a gruelling day, Cynthia realised that the elderly couple who had lived in the cottage for as long as they could remember had not been in for their usual weekly provisions. She asked Bernard to go and see if they were alright but he was unable to get any response to repeated knocks on their door. The police were called and forced an entry through a window at the back of the cottage. Upstairs they found a gas fire turned on but not alight and presumed the couple had committed suicide. However, at the inquest, Bernard's parents told the coroner they knew the couple well, from when they were neighbours, and considered it most unlikely they would have wanted to take their own lives. The police reported that one of the bedroom windows was wide open when they entered the room and the coroner said it seemed probable that the fire had been blown out by a gust of wind. After taking further evidence, the coroner recorded a verdict of death by misadventure.

There were no known surviving relatives and no will was ever produced. The victims had little money and relied upon their pensions for subsistence. Harry thought they owned the cottage, but when a rent book was discovered among their possessions it transpired that the premises belonged to a businessman in Belgium.

Bernard took it upon himself to write to the owner and break the news about his tenant. His fear of having a supermarket on his doorstep was now dwarfed by the prospect of having a stranger living in the house next door.

Others in the village were distressed at the thought of what could happen when you go to bed at night, and many of them rushed to convert from gas to electricity, but once the funeral had taken place it was not long before life in the village returned to normal. Cynthia summed it up when she said you could miss people when they moved or were not around but when they were dead in the churchyard you knew they had gone for ever.

Bernard's parents took longer to get over the tragedy because when they ran the *General Stores* they had been on good terms with their neighbours and were the only people in the village who ever had much to do with them. Even so, they knew little about their personal affairs and were surprised to find how poor they had been. It was evident that what the couple lacked in money they made up in pride by concealing their poverty.

Three weeks after the funeral Bernard received a letter saying the owner of the cottage was coming over, and asking if the premises would be in a suitable condition for him to stay there for a few days. Cynthia said 'no chance', but Bernard urged her to think about it. He offered to ask his mother if she would be prepared to go in and make the place habitable.

'We can lend some linen if necessary,' said Bernard, 'and set him up with food. Maybe we could do a deal with him while he's here.'

'What sort of deal had you in mind?' asked Cynthia, sarcastically. 'You weren't thinking of buying him out, were you?'

Bernard had not been thinking along those lines at all, but the idea struck him as eminently sensible. They had made more money from the sale of their suburban bungalow than the cottage was worth, and still had most of that money left, since the shop had been gifted to them as an inheritance. But would the owner want to sell?

Bernard tried to put the thought from his mind, but the prospect of joining the two buildings together was too appealing to go away. It would mean he could enlarge the shop and provide more living space for the family now that the children were growing up.

He could see from Cynthia's expression that her thoughts were not on the same wavelength.

When he spoke to his mother she suggested that instead of making the cottage fit for its owner to stay in, she and Harry could put him up on the spare bed in their house. It would be less trouble, she said, and more comfortable for the Belgian than sleeping in a damp and draughty building that had not been lived in since his tenants died. This was not what Bernard had asked for and he disliked the idea of his elderly parents having to cope with a boarder who probably spoke a foreign language. He decided to ask Cynthia if one of their children could sleep on the floor for a night so they could offer the Belgian a bed in their house.

'Certainly not!' said Cynthia. 'We haven't the facilities. Why don't you ask the publican if he'll do him bed and breakfast at the *Perch and Parrot*?'

Next morning Bernard arrived at the *Perch and Parrot*, not with his weekly delivery of groceries, but with an urgent and delicate mission. He knew that the village pub was no hotel, and doubted if the Perrymans had ever added bed and breakfast to their menu of beer and skittles, but in the circumstances he was ready to try them out.

Dick Perryman had managed the public house for longer than Bernard had been a shopkeeper and regarded his visitor as still a new boy to the neighbourhood. When Bernard told him his reason for calling, he explained that no-one in Backwater had ever needed anywhere to lodge their guests, so he'd never thought of running a guest house.

'I daresay that was true once,' said Bernard, 'but times are changing and I've had a request from a Belgian businessman to find him somewhere to stay while he looks over the house next to mine. We'd put him up ourselves, except that we haven't a spare room to offer him.'

Dick wondered if there was a business interest in the Belgian's visit and asked Bernard if he was thinking of selling the *General Stores*.

'Good heavens, no! Trade may be down a bit, but it's not that bad.'

'Well, I've got a room in the attic we keep furnished, though it's a long time since we had visitors. I can ask Winifred if she'll make it ready for you, if you like.'

Bernard thanked him and said he was sure the Belgian would be grateful.

As he turned to leave, Dick called him back.

'You didn't say if he spoke English.'

Bernard grinned.

'Neither did *he*! But his letter was in English, so if he doesn't speak it you can always ask him to write down what he wants.'

On the way out Bernard observed the pre-war décor of the bars and the framed units of stuffed fish and parrot on the walls. He wondered if he was right to be so sure about the Belgian's gratitude, but when he got home he wrote and told him there would be room for him to stay at an inn in the village as the house he owned was not yet in a fit state to be occupied.

Bernard and Cynthia were both behind the counter when a Mr Fletcher walked into the shop. He was not the stout, elderly Belgian they had envisaged but a slim, well-dressed Englishman in his early forties. He introduced himself apologetically and said he had taken their advice and booked a room at the *Perch and Parrot*. Cynthia blushed at the thought of being responsible for this and gave him the key to his cottage with an invitation to call on her if she could be of any help. He hesitated for a moment, then asked if she would be kind enough to show him round the cottage.

'I have never been in there,' he said, 'so I have no idea what to expect.'

Bernard said there was nothing to be afraid of as they had buried the bodies, but he nodded his approval for Cynthia to go with him and she led the way. When she returned to the *Stores*, forty minutes later, she told Bernard Mr Fletcher was a very nice man.

'I've invited him to join us at supper after we close the shop.'

That evening they listened across the dining table while Mr Fletcher told them his story. His father, he said, had bought the house for his grandmother when she was widowed during the First World War, but she had died before being able to move into it.

'My father was an engineer with a house of his own in Belgium, so he decided to rent it to a young couple who were looking for somewhere to live in the village. It seems they may have been the couple who died there. My father did say he would like us to live there one day, but before he was ready to retire, the Second World War had begun and we were stranded in Belgium. When that war ended *my* mother was a widow, but she did not want to start a new life among strangers in another country, so it suited us to leave tenants in the cottage and collect a modest rent.'

Bernard decided he liked Mr Fletcher, and knew already that Cynthia shared his opinion. Their feelings were a mixture of sympathy and admiration, and they would not have minded if he told them he was thinking of coming to live there himself. So they asked him if he was married.

'Oh, yes,' he said, 'and we have three young children.'

'Do they go to school?' asked Cynthia.

'Of course!' he replied.

'In Belgium?' asked Cynthia.

'Naturally,' said Mr Fletcher, 'why do you ask?'

'We were wondering,' Bernard confided, 'if you might be thinking of moving into the cottage yourselves, now that it is empty.'

'I don't think so,' came the reply. 'The cottage is in excellent condition but it's much too small for us, even as a holiday home. I daresay we'll put it on the market, but if we can't sell it we may try to find another tenant.'

There was a moment's silence, and Bernard looked meaningfully at Cynthia. Mr Fletcher caught sight of that look.

'I suppose,' he ventured, 'if you don't mind me asking, you wouldn't be interested in buying it, would you?'

Bernard gave a poor impression of never having thought of such a thing and said he would have to talk it over with his wife. Mr Fletcher said that was perfectly correct and understandable. Later that evening he returned to the *Perch and Parrot* reasonably confident he had secured a sale.

Confidence in the outcome of their meeting was not, however, shared in the Talbot household. Bernard was certainly pleased to find the way open for him to bid for the cottage but had no idea how much Fletcher would ask for it. Cynthia, who had put the idea into Bernard's head facetiously, wondered what they would do with it if they were to buy it. They discussed the matter well into the night and were no nearer a solution when they opened shop in the morning.

There was no dispute between them as to the usefulness of having more space in which to stock and display their goods, but they could think of no way of joining the two buildings together.

'Perhaps we should move our household belongings into the cottage, then we could extend the shop over the rest of the house.'

'Can you see any of our customers wanting to go up those stairs to do their shopping?'

'We could build them an escalator!'

'Dear Bernard, I doubt if we are ready yet to become a department store!'

It was fun while it lasted, but they both knew if a supermarket came to the area their turnover would fall, and the need for more space would disappear.

That evening, after Mr Fletcher had made a second visit to the cottage, Bernard suggested to Cynthia that he might ask his parents if they would like to move into the cottage.

'It would mean we could think of taking holidays, and have some back-up in case of sickness.'

Cynthia remembered the reservations she had previously expressed, but her resolve had weakened since she took over the *Stores* and she could now see the benefit of such an arrangement. The question was, would Harry and Mildred want to come back?

Bernard went to see them. It was clear that they were not really happy in the cottage they were renting and the idea of moving back to a place of their own had many attractions but Harry said he did not have enough money to buy it.

'We've got money left over from the sale of our bungalow,' said Bernard, 'and Cynthia and I would be happy to buy it for you, if you and mother would like to live there. After all, you did give us the house as well as the shop, remember.'

'That was to save paying tax when we die! Just now, you'll need all the money you've got to tide you over when trade gets rough, as it will if the supermarket appears.'

'Suppose we do a deal?' said Bernard, who was fond of that expression. 'I'll put up the capital and buy the cottage, but you and mother can pay us rent while you're living there. That way you'll be free to move on at any time without the hassle of selling.'

'Like when we die,' said his mother, picking up his father's remark, and being practical as ever.

'Forget about dying' said Bernard, 'but make sure you like the idea of living on our doorstep before you say yes.'

'There's just one condition,' said Mildred, being even more practical, 'and that is that we go on living separate lives and don't hop in and out of each other's doorways – unless invited!'

Bernard reported back to Cynthia who went straight down to her mother-in-law to accept the condition and say how pleased she was that they would soon be next-door neighbours as well as close relations. A price was agreed with Mr Fletcher and matters were placed in the hands of solicitors. A sale agreement was drawn up and, in due course, contracts were exchanged. Harry and Mildred gave notice to their landlord and moved their belongings into Primrose Cottage, next door to the *General Stores*.

Chapter 7

The return of Harry and Mildred to the vicinity of the *General Stores* brought back to the shop a few customers who had deserted when Bernard and Cynthia took over. It also created enough interest in the village for the local newspaper to carry a feature article describing the history of the Talbot family. This reopened the debate about the effect which a supermarket was likely to have on the future of the village stores.

Bernard made sure copies of the article were distributed as widely as possible. He gave one to every customer with their shopping, but a week later news broke that the council had given permission for a supermarket to be built on a new site even nearer to Backwater than the one originally proposed. An advertisement duly appeared inviting applications for staff to work there and, without saying a word to her father, Amy applied for a job.

Building work began immediately and Bernard realised it was now useless to continue his campaign of opposition. For a few days he considered the possibility of taking disruptive action, like people he had read about who tried to prevent new roads being built over picturesque countryside. On reflection he decided supermarkets were not in the same category as motorways and were unlikely to excite the same degree of public support. Instead, he resolved to embark upon a passive form of resistance. He would encourage more and more villagers to use their local shops and, if that failed, find ways to deter them from shopping elsewhere.

First, he must make sure that he and his fellow retailers could offer at least as good a service as people would get in the supermarket. It would then help if he could show that the difference in their prices did not exceed in aggregate what it would cost to get to the supermarket.

When he put this proposition to Old Doughie and Butch they made suitable gestures of support, but showed a preference for concentrating on deterrence rather than trying to outperform the opposition.

45

'We could put carts across the road so people can't get out of the village,' said Butch.

Doughie took him seriously. 'How'd our suppliers get in if we did that?' he asked.

Bernard dismissed the negative approach and suggested they took their time to think of some better ideas later.

'I'm going to start a programme of customer appeal,' he said. 'I mean to make people feel happy when they go shopping in the village.'

'How will you do that?' asked Butch. 'Tickle 'em with a duster, or spray 'em with laughing gas?'

'I shall put a banner over the front door,' said Bernard, 'saying *Welcome to the Friendly Store.*'

Doughie said he would do the same, but thought *Come here for your Daily Bread* might be more apt. Bernard thought it might offend the vicar.

Butch couldn't think of a slogan but said he would offer his customers mints to suck on the way out. Doughie said that would make them think they had bad breath, and insult those who hadn't.

Neither of them believed they would convince their customers it was cheaper to shop in the village, but Butch said he would increase his prices now so he could put them down later when the supermarket opened.

Bernard was determined not to go down without a fight. Whatever happened to the butcher and baker (and he was beginning to wonder how long they would survive now that the die had been cast) he was going to keep the *General Stores* open as long as there were people in the village with money to spend. And so long as he had money to spend he was going to invest it in the business. He would urge Cynthia to overcome her prudence and buy a new dress to wear in the shop; and he would insist that they both wore white aprons overprinted with the words 'At your Service'.

He told Cynthia he would place a suggestions box near the doorway inviting customers to ask for anything they wanted but did not see, and complain if there was anything they did not like. Cynthia said it presupposed they were hiding things and actually doing something objectionable, but Bernard insisted it would give the impression they were running the *Stores* to suit the customer.

'Which is more than can be said of the supermarkets which are in business to make a profit.'

Amy had been listening in the background. 'Aren't we going to make any profit then' she asked?

'Not if your father spends money the way he's talking about,' said Cynthia.

'It pays to advertise', said Bernard. Then, mixing his metaphors, he added 'sometimes it's worth using a sprat to catch a mackerel!'

Still on the theme of customer appeal, he said he would play music in the shop when business was slack.

'We'll run an extension speaker from our radiogram and hang it over the counter in the shop. Then we can chalk titles of our records on a notice board, like the menu in public houses where they sell food as a supplement to beer. That way people can choose what they want to hear while they're buying groceries. Didn't Shakespeare say something about music being a food?'

'Maybe,' said Cynthia, 'but he didn't have to listen to what they call music today.'

Cynthia's lack of enthusiasm did not stop Bernard putting his plan into operation. The reaction from customers was mixed. Some liked the idea and listened long enough to buy more than they might otherwise have done. Some even pretended to dance or sing to the numbers they selected. Others hurried from the shop, surrounded by sounds they found distasteful. Bernard was teased, and asked if he planned to sell hi-fi equipment and musical instruments, but many thanked him for making their shopping expeditions more interesting. The experiment was fun while it lasted, but the novelty wore off long before the records wore out.

Cynthia, meanwhile, continued to deal with the daily routines of shop-keeping and domesticity. Secretly she agreed with customers who said they missed the way things used to be and wished they could put the clock back. In public she backed her husband's ideas and admired his enterprise, but his next proposal put her loyalty to the test.

In a bid to raise more revenue he planned to hold a weekly sweepstake, convinced he would sell enough tickets to more than cover the cost of a prize. Unfortunately, his gamble was doomed from the start because he discovered such a scheme would amount to a lottery and require a licence. To keep within the law he had to reduce the element of chance. So, instead of charging people for a ticket he gave his customers a numbered receipt for their purchases and drew one of the numbers each week to win a prize. The expense of buying printed receipt books was more than offset by the extra business generated and because the prize was always awarded in kind, the cost of that was only marginal. Moreover, it helped to clear some of the slow-moving items and made room on the shelves for a wider variety of products. This helped Cynthia concede that the game was worth playing.

Prize-giving became a popular event and made Tuesdays a busier day in the shop than hitherto.

One day a new customer walked in to the shop when Cynthia was behind the counter.

'I'm so pleased to find a shop in the village where I can buy food and household goods,' she said. 'My husband and I have just moved in to a nice house not far from here. He is going to manage the new supermarket but until it opens it is nice to know I shall be able to do my shopping here.'

Cynthia stared at her with a mixture of anger and astonishment. How could the woman be so insensitive? Instinctively she wanted to tell the woman she was unwelcome, and show her the door, but her better judgement told her to sink her pride and sell the stranger as much as possible. Reluctantly, Cynthia chose to be polite. The lady bought a week's supply of everything she needed for the house, and said she would call again next week. As she was leaving, Cynthia asked her where in the village she was living. Her reply added further irony, for she said they were renting the farm cottage from which Harry and Mildred had recently moved.

Bernard gasped when Cynthia told him the news.

'Spying on us, was she! I'll make her sorry for that. You let me serve her next time she comes in.'

'I doubt if many spies would declare themselves as she did. Don't you think we'd do better to cultivate her and make the most of her custom while it lasts?'

Bernard did think about it, and then had an idea of his own.

'Perhaps we can turn her into a double agent!' he chuckled.

That evening, when Bernard reported the incident to George Trotter, the butcher gave him another surprise.

'I hear that daughter o' yours is going to work there when it opens,' he said.

'Who said so?'

'Oh, Lor', have I put m' foot in it? Didn't y' know? Daphne didn't say it were a secret.'

Amy was out when Bernard wanted to speak to her, so he turned on Cynthia.

'Did you know Amy had lined up a job at the supermarket?'

'Yes', said Cynthia. 'Didn't she tell you?'

'You know darn well she didn't, or you'd have mentioned it!'

'Sorry, I must have forgotten.'

The timely return of their daughter helped to avert a matrimonial rift. Amy could see from the look on her father's face that she had been rumbled. A hint from her friend Daphne had forewarned her of the discovery.

'Did I tell you, Dad? They've offered me a job when the new supermarket opens. I'll be able to bring you inside information about what goes on there.'

Her mother was about to intervene when Bernard surprised them both by holding out his hand and offering congratulations.

'How much are they going to pay you?' he asked. Then, before she could answer, he added: 'whatever it is, it will do nicely for the rent!'

Amy was inwardly hurt, but quick to respond.

'OK,' she said, ' then I'll charge you for spying on them.'

'I wish you and your father would stop talking about spying,' said Cynthia, 'I'm sure it's illegal.'

Bernard and Amy looked doubtfully at each other, and then laughed.

Contractors now began to move on to the site and squads of building workers were engaged for the various tasks of construction. Most of the workers came from other parts of the country, and some from abroad, so nearly all of them looked for accommodation in the neighbourhood. Some came to Backwater where villagers with rooms to spare took in lodgers and were glad of the extra money. More goods were sold in the *General Stores*, and elsewhere in the village, and business flourished ahead of the impending recession.

However, not all the traders were as realistic as Bernard. Some borrowed money in anticipation of rising profits without regard to the ephemeral nature of the upturn. The sudden popularity of sandwiches caused Doughie to buy a larger oven to cope with the huge demand for bread, and Bobby Burns installed a new pump at the filling station to meet the increased sales of petrol. Bernard knew the day would come when the temporary residents would depart, and opposition from the new marketplace would reduce business in the village, but even he had to call for bigger and faster delivery of supplies to keep up with the current demand.

The enjoyment of such unprecedented business soon gave rise to greed, and Bernard was not exempt from such avarice. He realised they could sell even more if the shops were open on Sundays. Many of the construction workers had time to spare at weekends yet there was little for them to do in the village. Dick Perryman, the publican, was making a fortune at the *Perch and Parrot,* and Bobby Burns was busier than ever at the pumps, but the butcher, baker and *General Stores* were shut.

Cynthia was against any extension of the working week and said she was working hard enough from Monday to Saturday. Bernard agreed that she deserved a day off but suggested they could take it in turns to open the shop on Sundays.

'That would still mean working 13 out of every 14 days,' said Cynthia, 'which is too much.'

Bernard said he was not superstitious, but Cynthia was serious.

Thinking they would be doing a favour, Harry and Mildred offered to cover for them on one day of the week, and it looked as though the matter might be settled - until the vicar heard about it.

The Rev Vernon Lovelock was not a regular customer at the *General Stores*. He had called there once or twice for biscuits or milk, when unexpected visitors arrived at the Rectory, but his appearance at the shop, in round collar and cassock, was a surprise. It brought to an abrupt end a conversation Bernard was having with his wife and, since neither was normally among his congregation, they were curious to know what he had come for.

'Good morning,' said the vicar, cheerfully. 'I hope I'm not disturbing you, but I wondered if we might have a word, privately.'

Bernard asked Cynthia to look after the shop while he and the vicar went into the back room so as not to be disturbed.

'Well, no,' said the vicar, 'I should like you both to hear what I have to say.'

Bernard glanced at his wife and feared it might have something to do with their son or daughter.

'If it's got to be private', he said, 'we'd better make an appointment for when the shop is closed. Could you call again this evening, or would you like us to come to the vicarage?'

The Rev Lovelock looked confused, but said he would call again 'after working hours.'

True to his word, he went back to the shop that evening and explained his mission.

'The Book says,' he began, 'that on the seventh day there shall be a day of rest. So when I heard you were thinking of opening the *Stores* on Sundays I felt I owed it to my parishioners to ask you, well, to think again.'

Cynthia was about to conciliate, but Bernard had other views.

'Do you ever take a train, or buy a newspaper on a Sunday?' he asked.

The vicar had expected opposition.

'Yes, of course. I know what you are going to say, but there is a difference between working on essential services for the benefit of other people, and working unnecessarily in order - well, shall we say, for the sake of expediency - to permit the luxury of buying goods that could be bought on other days.'

'Or, were you going to say, in order to make more money?'

'Mr Talbot, I did not wish to be offensive, for I am sure your motive is not as base as that. But I do hope you will see that opening the shop on Sundays would create a most undesirable precedent which others might exploit for a variety of motives.'

'Mr Lovelock, I appreciate your concern for protecting those who might be tempted to do what you regard as immoral, but I have to remind you there are others in this world who have to work when shops are open during the week and need somewhere to buy their necessities on Sundays.'

'Necessities, perhaps, but don't you think many people would regard it as an opportunity to treat Sunday like any other day of the week?'

'Maybe, but let me ask you another question. Shortly there will be a new supermarket in the area; will you be able to stop that opening on Sundays?'

'I will certainly try to, but unfortunately it will not be in my parish.'

'Then, let me put the question another way. If, when that supermarket opens, all your parishioners go there to shop during the week and I have to close the *General Stores* because I cannot afford to keep it open, what will you do for those people in the village who have not got the means to travel to the supermarket? Pray for them, I suppose!'

The Rev Lovelock said he was praying now that the *General Stores* would remain open – 'six days of the week, but not on Sundays.'

Chapter 8

The day the supermarket opened was, for Bernard, the day war broke out. And, like it was in England in 1939, there followed a period of relative inactivity, described then as 'the phoney war'. After an abrupt drop in business, when the construction workmen left, trade soon levelled off and villagers in Backwater continued to shop locally until, imperceptibly, custom began to slacken and stocks to move more slowly. At Blackie's Garage, sales plummeted when the workmen left but picked up steadily as more people from the village filled their cars with petrol on their way to the supermarket.

Anxious to hold on to as much business as possible, Bernard and Cynthia painted their delivery van on both sides with the words LET'S KEEP IT IN THE VILLAGE. (The slogan was meant to encourage people to shop locally but was regarded by many as a pious attempt to avoid being robbed.)

George Trotter did his best to improve business in the butcher's shop by laying out his cuts of meat in a new display cabinet and wearing a new blue-striped apron with a large white floppy hat. He also hung on the wall a framed certificate to advertise his prizewinning sausages.

Doughie produced an increased variety of cakes, and introduced a long twisted loaf, which he described as French but baked from the same dough as the rest of his bread.

Meanwhile, eight miles from Backwater, in company with many girls from neighbouring villages, Amy started work at the supermarket. The manager, Mr Grimley, fitted them out with smart uniforms, designed with the company's colours, placed them at counters called check-outs, and gave them instructions how to operate the tills. Many, like Amy, were young teenagers eager to earn their own living for the first time, and some were part-timers still at school. Wages were low, but working conditions were reasonable, and they were all grateful to have a job. During the early part of the day when business was slack they endured periods of stark monotony, but once the store got busy there was no time to be bored.

At the end of her first day at work Amy found her father waiting for her when she got home.

'Well, young lady', he asked 'what have you learned that you couldn't have learned working with us in the *General Stores*?'

'Lots of things,' she said. 'People buy more there than they do in here. They like pushing those trolleys around, and I'm sure they fill them up with far more than they really need: there are so many 'special offers' they can't resist. If a packet says it contains ten percent more of something they'll buy it because it sounds like a bargain, but I bet if it said the price had been reduced by ten percent they'd think it had something wrong with it.'

The floodgates were open and she was still talking when it was time to go to bed.

Bernard knew that Amy's experience at a check-out would add little to what he remembered from when he was a supermarket customer himself, but he hoped she would bring home some tips about what people were now buying, and how much they were prepared to spend on a single shopping expedition. Eventually, after she had been in the job for a month or two, she was able to tell him which products were in constant demand, and he was able to increase stocks in the *General Stores* accordingly. Sometimes, however, his hope of selling more was dashed because he could not compete with the supermarket's price.

When Amy told her parents they were stocking items in the *General Stores* which were not sold at all in the supermarket they were faced with a different problem. Instead of disposing of the stocks cheaply, her mother hit upon the idea of advertising them as *Goods for the discerning customer*, adding the incentive that they were *unavailable elsewhere in the district*. The gimmick worked occasionally, but when it did not, and the goods remained unsold for more than a week, Bernard complained that space on the shelves had been lost for products which might have proved more popular.

As many others have discovered, it is one thing to have access to inside information but not always possible to put it to good use. On one occasion, when Amy told him how much they were charging in the supermarket for a popular brand of washing-up liquid, Bernard undercut its price in the *General Stores*, only to find the supermarket chose the following day to promote it as a loss-leader and reduced its price even further. On another occasion when he removed stocks of a product because Amy said it was 'a slow-mover', it appeared in a televised advertisement and became a best seller. By the time he got a new supply the advertisement had been forgotten and Bernard was left with more than he had in the first place.

Sometimes, when he heard of goods that were selling well in the supermarket, Bernard wanted to display them as 'special offers' in the *General Stores*. This invariably led to an argument. Bernard said they would sell more and customers would see they could buy things as cheaply in the village as at the supermarket. Cynthia said if something was in great demand in the supermarket there would be a market for it in the village anyway and there was no point in losing profit by selling it more cheaply. It was ironic, therefore, that when they did succeed in selling more by cutting their price they were frequently unable to keep up with demand and alienated customers who found them out of stock.

Such incidents were not the only sources of frustration, for Bernard realised the supermarket offered many facilities that were simply not available to his customers. He tried to compensate in a small way by introducing wire baskets and trolleys for carrying goods to waiting cars, but he knew that the one facility he could not hope to provide was a designated car park. It was a defect he had not envisaged when he took over the establishment and it became the topic of conversation at their dinner table on Sundays for many weeks to come.

It would have pleased him to be able to share these burdens with his son, but Jonathan was not interested. Since leaving school he had begun a course of mechanical engineering at the Regional Technical College and at weekends had a part-time job at Blackie's Garage helping in the workshop or on the petrol pumps.

One summer evening, on his way home from the garage, he took a short cut across the fields and was surprised to see his sister's friend, Daphne, approaching on horseback.

'Hallo,' she said when she was close enough to recognise him. 'You're Amy's brother, aren't you?'

'Yes,' he replied.

'Do you like horses?' she asked.

'No,' he said, bluntly.

'What *do* you like?' she asked.

Jonathan hesitated. He *dis*liked her tone of voice. It sounded haughty.

'Mice', he said.

'Mice?' she repeated.

'Well, one in particular.'

She looked surprised, thinking perhaps he kept one in a cage.

'What colour is it?'

'White.'

'Really! Where do you keep it?'

'Next to my computer.'

Her heels struck sharply into the horse, and they galloped off across the field.

Jonathan stood watching them, then turned and continued his walk home. A few moments later he heard the horse returning and looked up to find Daphne staring down at him from the saddle.

'I'm going your way now. Can I give you a lift?'

'No thanks, I'd rather walk.'

'Please yourself', she said and galloped off again, this time racing ahead of him towards a gate at the end of the field. It was a large field that led directly on to the road almost opposite her father's shop.

Jonathan put his head down and walked on, but after a few yards he stopped and looked up to see Daphne leading her horse through the gate. He remembered her remark about giving him a lift, and the idea of her stopping to pick up a passenger amused him. Where would she have expected him to sit if he had accepted the offer? How would he have got on, and where would she have put him off? The image of a horse merged in his mind with that of the motor cycle they were repairing at the garage and that, in turn, mutated into a two-seater sports car. He saw himself being driven by Daphne through open country to a far off destination, but the fantasy faded as he remembered what his father had been saying about wanting a car park for customers of the *General Stores*. Suddenly he could visualise the field being stacked with vehicles where a moment ago a horse and its rider had passed.

When he reached home Jonathan went straight to his father and shyly explained what had occurred to him as he walked across the field. He made no mention of meeting the butcher's daughter, but said the size and position of the field made him think of it as a possible site for a car park.

Bernard confessed he may have judged the boy too harshly.

'What a splendid idea!' he said.

Without delay he set off for *The Brambles*, to see the man who owned the field that Jonathan had crossed.

'It's not for sale,' said Butch.

'Then let me rent it from you,' Bernard pleaded.

'What do you want it for?'

Bernard explained.

'I might think about it,' said Butch who saw that his business might also benefit from a car park. 'P'raps we could leave the gate open so your customers and mine could drive in when the shops are open.'

A deal was struck and it worked well for both parties for the rest of the summer. While the weather was fine there was room in the field for all their customers, but later in the year when it rained they had more trouble getting the cars out than getting them in.

Chapter 9

Mr Grimley did not take long to settle into his role as manager of the new supermarket, for he had been in training as assistant manager at another branch of the same company. He was, however, unaccustomed to living in the country and the people thereabouts were different to those he had dealt with in the suburbs; a fact that he was slow to recognise. The impression he gave to his new customers was that he was only interested in making a profit for his employers. He was either unaware or unconcerned that the supermarket might be seen as a threat to other traders in the area, and confident enough to suppose there was no local retailer who could offer any serious competition. He engaged staff from nearby villages without regard to their social background, and had no idea that one of his check-out clerks was the daughter of a local trader.

Mrs Grimley continued to do her shopping at the *General Stores* in Backwater, partly because she could not rely on her husband to bring home all the goods she needed and partly because she liked the friendliness of those she met there. In spite of their initial reservations, the Talbots resolved to cultivate her custom, but were anxious not to reveal they had a daughter working in the supermarket. They feared that one of their other customers might mention it when Mrs Grimley was in the shop but whenever the conversation looked likely to lead to such a revelation they quickly changed the subject.

Amy, meanwhile, was making friends with other girls in the supermarket. Her father warned her not to tell any of them exactly where she lived, or what her father did for a living. It might not have pleased him, but she bent the truth enough to protect him by telling them she rarely saw her father because he was a long-distance lorry driver and often away when she got home.

Jonathan had no problem with the content of his conversations for he was not gregarious and rarely talked to anyone in the village, even when he was working at the garage. He did, however, think a lot and frequently turned over in his mind the encounter with Daphne and her horse. At the time his feelings towards her had been no more than an awareness that she was a friend of his sister, but he was beginning to realise there was something else about her which appealed to him. Perhaps it was her remark about giving him a lift because it was that which led to his thinking of turning her father's field into a car park. He certainly owed her some gratitude for that as it brought about a closer relationship with his father. On reflection, he felt an urge to meet her again.

So, when his mother mentioned on Friday that she was going to the butchers for their weekend joint, Jonathan offered to save her the trouble and said he would get it for her.

'That's very kind of you,' she said, 'but it's never been any trouble before.'

'It's just that …' Jonathan stammered, '…I thought I'd like to see what goes on in a butcher's shop.'

'I don't suppose it's much different to what goes on in this shop except, of course, they sell meat there,' said his mother. 'But, if there's something else you want to see, by all means go. Only don't forget to bring back the Sunday joint!'

Jonathan turned to go and to hide his blushes, but much to his disappointment when he reached the butchers, Daphne was not around. It was her mother who served him.

'Don't often see you here, do we, lad?' said Mrs Trotter. 'Is your mother not well?'

Embarrassed, but not deterred, Jonathan said his mother was fine but asked if Daphne was all right.

'Why, goodness, yes,' said Mrs Trotter, surprised to be asked. 'She's away in the field, with Archibald.'

'Oh, I see.'

'Archie is the horse. In case you didn't know!'

'Oh, yes. I've met him.'

'Well, if you go across the road opposite you'll find them both over there.'

What Jonathan found across the road was only half a field as he remembered it. The gate to the road was open and there was a car parked neatly inside, behind the hedge. Across the middle of the field were posts and a long rope on which a notice was hung saying *PRIVATE (Reserved for horse.)* Beyond that he caught sight of Daphne riding Archibald.

On seeing Jonathan she galloped towards him.

'Hallo,' she shouted, 'how's the mouse these days?'

'Fine. What about the horse?'

'Oh, is that who you came to see? Archie's fine. Lots more fun than your mouse!'

'I didn't know he had a name.'

'What do you call your mouse?'

'Micky!' he lied.

'Oh no, not that! What do you feed it with?'

'Electricity.'

'How shocking!'

Jonathan laughed. 'Would you like to touch him?'

He pulled from his pocket a piece of mechanical equipment which he had earlier detached from its usual connection to a computer.

Daphne dismounted and took the instrument in her hand. Pretending to fondle it, she placed it back in Jonathan's hand, deliberately touching his flesh with her fingers as she did so. For the first time in his life he felt the magical sensation of sex.

Sunday's lunch tasted sweet that weekend, and Cynthia detected a glint in her son's eye which told her more than she would have learned if she had asked him why he took so long to return from the butcher.

Before lunch that day Amy had been out riding, so she knew of Daphne's meeting with Jonathan, but said nothing about it to her mother. Such sibling sensitivity was unusual, but Amy had a reason to be discreet. She had recently met a young man at the supermarket who had been in Jonathan's class at school and she was anxious to keep the friendship secret from her parents. After lunch, she took Jonathan to one side and asked him what he thought of Daphne.

'I liked her better than her horse,' he replied.

'I should jolly well hope so,' said Amy. 'She likes you, you know.'

Jonathan blushed again and went back to his computer.

Amy's friend at the supermarket was employed as a stock-keeper and his job was to take deliveries from the unloading bay, stack them in the stockroom and dispense them around the store as the shelves became empty. Amy realised he was in a good position to tell her where the goods were coming from and asked him to make a note of some of the suppliers.

'What do you want to know that for?' he asked, not unreasonably.

'Cos I think my dad might want to do business with them.'

She had promised her father not to let any of her friends at work know of her connection with the *General Stores*, but knew that Freddie had been one of her father's Banner Boys and felt it was safe to confide in him.

'You helped my dad once, didn't you?' she said. 'That was before the supermarket opened. I reckoned you might want to help him again now.'

'Yes, of course I would, but I don't see what use I can be now I'm working there'

'I think you can, because he wants to buy his supplies from the same source as the supermarket.'

'He'll never be able to compete with them, will he?'

'You don't know my dad!'

'Oh yes I do, and he's a nice man. If you think I can help him, I will.'

Freddie was no sycophant, but he could see a way to Amy's favour.

Bernard was delighted when Amy told him the supermarket was being supplied with a range of soft fruit and spring vegetables by a Farmer Berry who owned land on the edge of the village. Freddie had told her the farmer was an irascible character, known locally as 'Prickly' Berry, who made a living in one half of the year and spent it in the other. His fortune varied with the weather, for too much rain or frost and too little sunshine, reduced his income and ruined his temper.

When Bernard went to see him it had been a mild winter. With nothing like the purchasing power of a retailing giant, Bernard invited him to sell as much of his produce as possible through the *General Stores*.

'I'll pay you more than you get from the supermarket,' Bernard assured him.

'In pounds, or total?'

'Per pound.'

'How much will you sell?'

'I don't know, but what I can't take you could sell elsewhere.'

'You mean you want first call?'

'Yes.'

'Why should I do that when I can sell everything I produce to the supermarket?'

'Because if I can't keep my customers happy they'll go to the supermarket, and if people stop shopping in the village I'll soon be out of business.'

'Sounds like you want to put *me* out of business. If the Big Boys get to know I'm selling to you, they'll look for another supplier.'

'They need never know. I could collect at night.'

'What, with that van with your name all over it?'

'All right. You deliver it in your truck to a quiet spot and I'll pick it up later.'

'Prickly' said he'd think about it.

'I could make it worth your while in other ways,' said Bernard as a parting shot. 'You'd earn the gratitude of many pensioners who can't get to the supermarket.'

Farmer Berry was a businessman and not a philanthropist, but the idea of making more money on even a small quantity and doing a good deed to the community at the same time appealed to him. A deal was struck.

Mr Grimley was surprised when his wife brought home a basket of freshly gathered raspberries and presented them with cream for his supper.

'How splendid!' he remarked. 'Have you been fruit picking?'

'No,' she said, 'I bought them in the *General Stores* at Backwater.'

'If you'd asked me I could have brought some home from the supermarket.'

He had no suspicion they had come from the same source.

Bernard could not resist telling George Trotter that he might be able to put him in touch with a farmer who supplied the supermarket with pork and poultry.

'What good'll that do me?' asked the butcher. 'Unless you think I could afford to buy him out.'

Bernard explained how he had secured supplies of fruit and vegetables.

Persuasion was never an easy option for Butch and he was less successful with Henry Duckworth, the livestock farmer, than Bernard had been with 'Prickly' Berry. Farmer Duckworth was already supplying him with a small number of chickens at weekends, and turkeys at christmas. Far from being willing to sell him more at a better price, he said he might soon be unable to sell him any at all. The supermarket, he said, was demanding more of his stock every month and it would put him out of business if he lost their order.

'That's what the fruit farmer said to me,' said Bernard when he heard. 'Didn't you tell him he would soon be putting *you* out of business if he sold all his produce to the supermarket?'

'Bernard! That man makes his living out of killing animals. He's not likely to care much if he knocks me out as well, now is he?'

Bernard had to admit it seemed unlikely.

When Daphne saw her father that evening he told her he had been asked by Bernard to do something which looked like cutting off entirely his supply of meat and poultry. Daphne asked him if it meant she ought to cut off her connections with the Talbot family.

'No, no,' said her father. 'It's got nothing to do with your friend Amy.'

But it was not her friendship with Amy that she was thinking about.

When Amy got home that evening, she told her father he looked as if he had had a bad day.

'I have,' he replied. 'I tried to get a butcher to draw blood out of a stone!'

Amy tried to envisage the attempt.

'I'm disappointed with Butch,' said Bernard. 'I passed on the information you got from your friend but he couldn't persuade the farmer to increase his supply of pork and poultry. In fact, he was told he soon won't be getting any at all because they'll all be going to the supermarket. If that happens we shan't have a butcher in the village much longer.'

Mr Grimley had never been to Backwater but knowing that his wife was in the habit of shopping there he said he would like to go with her one day.

'We can go on Sunday, if you like,' she said. 'The shop where I go has just started opening on Sundays.'

'Good, then we can buy some more raspberries,' he suggested.

Chapter 10

The weather was warm when Mr and Mrs Grimley drove into the village. They parked their car, as directed, in the field opposite the butcher's shop and walked a few yards further to the *General Stores*. Bernard was serving a customer as they entered, so he called for assistance. Amy responded, but seeing her manager in the doorway, stepped back quickly and pushed her mother forward. Cynthia recognised Mrs Grimley, and understood her daughter's panic. Mrs Grimley introduced her husband and Cynthia reciprocated when Bernard finished serving the customer.

Mr Grimley caught sight of Amy retreating, but as she was out of uniform and in her Sunday best he did not recognise her.

At intervals throughout the evening Arthur Grimley recalled the image of a young woman turning her back on him in the village shop. She was very pretty and he tried to remember where he had seen her before. Perhaps it was a face he had seen on the screen in a cinema, or on television, or maybe in a colour supplement to a Sunday newspaper. Or, was it in one of his wife's glossy magazines? He would have asked his wife to help him but feared she might detect that he had allowed his mind to wander. It bothered him to think he had been mentally unfaithful and physically aroused.

By the time he returned to work on Monday morning his mind was back on the tasks of management, but that afternoon, as he was passing the check-outs on a tour of the shop floor, his eyes fell on Amy and the vision of a bewitching village maiden returned. He felt dazed for a moment, as though he was still dreaming, but pulled himself together and was about to approach the check-out to confirm his suspicion (or exorcise the image) when a supervisor rushed towards him and directed his attention to a display cabinet in the fish department.

Nothing could have brought him back to reality more swiftly. Propped against the frame of a refrigerated cabinet was a large white card on which the following letters had been pasted, cut from a magazine or newspaper:

THESE FISH ARE POIS ON.

Grimley snatched the card from the cabinet, told his supervisor to close the department, and rushed into his office to telephone the police. While he was waiting for them to arrive a small group of customers hung around the cabinet watching it being emptied. Those who had read the notice before it was taken away passed on their interpretation of its meaning and they all left the shop resolved to buy fish elsewhere in future.

When the police arrived they asked the usual questions and took the card back to the station for analysis. Later that day two officers from the CID called to see the manager and described their suspicions.

'You do know, sir, I suppose,' said one of them to Mr Grimley, 'there are people in the neighbourhood who didn't want a supermarket to be built here and it's very likely they are still conducting their campaign against you.'

Mr Grimley had been told by his head office to expect some opposition when he took up his appointment, but the way the policeman said it made it sound threatening and rather personal.

'Do you have anyone in mind who might have been responsible?' he asked.

No one in particular, they said, but asked him if there was anyone on his staff who lived in the village of Backwater. Grimley could not remember, but sent for his supervisor who produced a staff list. When the names of Freddie and Amy were read out neither meant anything to him at that stage.

'I think you had better have them in for questioning,' the senior policeman suggested, adding dramatically, 'preferably one at a time.'

Mr Grimley asked his supervisor to fetch the young woman first.

When Amy was shown in she smiled sweetly and wondered why the manager's eyes were popping out of his head. Admiration rather than surprise was expressed by the plain-clothes policemen.

'Do...do you live in Backwater?' Mr Grimley stuttered.

Amy thought she was about to be rebuked for ignoring him on Sunday.

'It says here, on this address list,' said Mr Grimley, not waiting for Amy to answer, 'that you live at the *General Stores* in Backwater. Is that right?'

'Yes, sir. I suppose you saw me there yesterday. I'm sorry I didn't serve you, but I'm afraid I hadn't any make-up on and I was rather embarrassed.'

Mr Grimley struggled with his sentiments. This was the girl he had eulogised, and now he was being asked to believe she was a saboteur.

Observing that the manager was having difficulty interrogating the girl, one of the policemen showed Amy the card and asked her if she had seen it before.

Amy stared at it and shook her head.

'Can you tell us how it may have come to be on the fish counter?'

Amy looked surprised. 'I didn't put it there, if that's what you think,' she said.

'All right, but do you know who did, or anything about it?'

'No! Why should I?' she asked.

'Because you live in Backwater, and that's where there were demonstrations against the supermarket before it was built. Is that not so?'

'That was a long time ago, and I wouldn't be working here if I was still protesting, would I?'

It was an unfortunate remark for it reinforced Grimley's suspicion that she had been planted there to undermine the business and exact revenge. His dream of the village siren was now shattered. He thanked her politely and told her severely to go home until she heard from him again.

They then sent for Freddie, and when he was shown the card he burst out laughing.

'That don't look to me like a threat,' he told them. 'It's French.'

Mr Grimley and the policemen exchanged glances, but were not amused.

'So you know something about it, then?'

'I don't know how it got there, but I know what it means.'

'Perhaps you'll be good enough to tell us!'

'Well, it says these fish are fish. That's not surprising, is it? Poisson means fish in French.'

'What I see says poison, and that's what it means to anyone in English.'

'Maybe,' said Freddie, 'but that's because an S has fallen off.'

Mr Grimley and the policemen looked again at the card and agreed there was a gap between the S and O. But, they were still not amused.

'Since you know all about it,' said the policeman, 'you'd better tell us who did it.'

Freddie said he really didn't know but thought they ought to leave it to the police to find the culprits. They told him they were the police and took him down to the station where they threatened to charge him for withholding evidence. He was later given a lecture on wasting police time, and sent home.

Arthur Grimley made his report to Head Office from where he was told to discharge any member of staff who lived in Backwater and not to engage anyone from there in future.

Bernard was shocked to hear of Amy's dismissal, and realised it may have resulted from her attempts to spy for him in the supermarket. She assured him, however, that she knew nothing about the planting of a card on the fish cabinet. It cheered him to think that someone might have been trying to keep alive the campaign he had led to thwart the introduction of a supermarket, but it saddened him to think his daughter and her friend might have lost their job because of it. He asked Amy if she thought any of the Banner Boys had anything to do with it. Anxious to protect Freddie, she said she doubted if any of them could have been involved because all the young men employed by the supermarket worked outside the building.

When she next saw Freddie Amy told him of her father's suspicion. Freddie confessed he had told the boys that her father was trying to prevent the supermarket monopolising the output of local farmers and said he had encouraged them to think of ways to help.

'Truthfully,' said Freddie, 'I had no idea what they planned to do, but I have heard since that it was Tommy who designed and prepared the card and Lenny who slipped in during the lunch hour and placed it on the display cabinet when no-one was looking. They said they thought a fishy message might frighten off a few customers who were unfamiliar with the French language.'

Amy said, 'It probably frightened Old Grimley more than his customers.'

'When they heard we lost our jobs as a result of their exploit,' Freddie added, 'they wanted to confess so we'd get reinstated. But I told them it wouldn't make any difference. I said it's best to let Grimley think it might happen again.'

'What did they say to that?' Amy asked.

'Good idea! P'raps he'll hang around the meat and vegetable departments.'

Which reminded Freddie he had promised Amy to find out who was supplying the supermarket with potatoes. In the excitement he had forgotten to tell her.

Bernard was delighted to receive this last piece of intelligence and when Amy told him it was Freddie who had been her informer he said she should invite him to have lunch with them one day as a reward.

The farmer who owned fields where potatoes, swedes and turnips were being grown in the neighbouring village of Siley was Colonel Battersby-Edwards, a retired army officer, who had a reputation of being tough with trespassers and difficult to deal with. Bernard discovered he was also a regular churchgoer, which gave him the idea of seeking help from the vicar.

The Reverend Vernon Lovelock was as surprised to find Bernard at the vicarage as Bernard had been a few weeks earlier to see him at the *General Stores*.

Bernard's proposition was that the vicar should ask the farmer, in the interest of his parishioners, to divert a proportion of his crop to local traders.

'They need help,' said Bernard, 'to resist the encroachment of a monolithic retailing organisation which is undermining the very nature of the countryside'.

The Reverend Lovelock listened patiently but said he doubted if he could influence the Colonel on anything other than spiritual matters.

'After all,' he added, sourly, 'I evidently failed to persuade you not to open your shop on Sundays.'

Bernard smiled and said perhaps he would have more success with someone who was a member of his congregation.

The vicar agreed to mention it if he saw the Colonel.

'I suggest you leave it for a few days,' he told Bernard, 'and then call on him one evening at the farmhouse.'

Which is what he did, but when Bernard spoke to the Colonel it soon became clear that the vicar had given him only a vague impression of what he wanted.

'I understand,' said Colonel Battersby-Edwards 'that you have a philanthropic mission to feed the poor folk in these parts with a regular supply of vegetables.'

'Well, yes,' said Bernard, unsure how to proceed from there.

'Very noble of you!' said the Colonel. 'What is it you think I can do to help you?'

Bernard said he would like a regular supply of vegetables at a price he could afford.

'How do you propose to distribute them?'

Bernard explained that he would sell them to customers at the *General Stores*, and spare them from driving into town to buy them from the supermarket.

'Sell them! I thought you wanted to give them away!'

Bernard blushed.

'I'm not a financial philanthropist,' he told the Colonel. 'My mission, as you call it, is to keep the village shop open while the tide of business flows towards the supermarket.'

The Colonel weighed him up and decided he looked genuine.

'Do you think the tide will ebb one day and business return to the villages?'

'I would like to think so.'

'So would I,' said the Colonel, and invited Bernard into the farmhouse where he poured him a large tot of whisky from a heavy cutglass decanter.

An hour and two tots later, a deal had been struck. Bernard could buy from the farm, at no less than the supermarket paid, as much produce as he could sell in his shop for less than the supermarket were charging their customers.

When Bernard returned to the shop he was greeted by the unfamiliar sight of a horse tethered to the front gate. He asked himself if he had correctly totted up the number of tots he had imbibed with the Colonel or, maybe, underestimated the strength of the whisky. Cynthia could tell the meeting had gone well. Bernard's face was flushed and his expression cheerful; but it changed to a frown as he enquired about the horse.

'Jonathan has a visitor,' she told him.

'I didn't know he had a horse.'

'He hasn't. It's not his. It belongs to Amy's friend Daphne.'

'I thought you said it was Jonathan who had a visitor.'

'I did. She's called to see Jonathan.'

Bernard was slow to get the message.

'Where are they, then? I mean, Jonathan and Amy's friend. I know where the horse is!'

Cynthia said they were upstairs with the computer.

She had been busy in the shop when Daphne called and assumed she was another customer. When it came to her turn to be served Daphne said that Jonathan had promised to show her his mouse and she had come to see it.

Computer jargon was still new to Cynthia and her immediate reaction bordered on the hostile. However, the grin on Daphne's face was close enough to a smile to rescue her, and instead of being shown the door to the street she was directed to a door at the back of the shop which opened on to a flight of stairs leading to the attic. Cynthia was anxious to attend to another customer, and told her to call out when she got to the first landing.

'You'll find Jonathan on the next floor up,' she said, careful not to mention the word bedroom.

Jonathan was on the verge of making a record score in a computer game called 'Aliens from Outer Space'. An icon sped unaided along endless corridors, over unexpected obstacles and mind-boggling hazards, towards a virtually unreachable goal while invaders attacked from all directions. Jonathan's task was to repel the invaders. This required skilful finger work with a mouse or keyboard and extreme concentration, for he had to aim at targets coming on to the screen at great speed and shoot them down before they reached the roving icon. Thinking it was his mother calling to him from the floor below, he cursed the interruption and made no attempt to respond. Undeterred, Daphne continued upwards until she came to a door on which a badge depicting a motorcycle was attached. Satisfied she had reached her destination, she knocked.

'What do you want?' came the response.

'What have you got?' she shouted.

68

Jonathan jumped as he recognised the voice; just in time to see a bunch of hostile aliens burst on to the screen. He was too late to stop them killing the icon, and the game was brought to an abrupt end, ten points short of his previous maximum.

Daphne guessed from the look in his eyes as he opened the door that he was pleased to see her, but she could tell from the way he had answered her knock at the door that she had interrupted something important.

'Never mind,' he protested. 'I'll have another go tomorrow.'

'Why not now?' she asked.

Jonathan did not like to say he would be unable to concentrate with her in the room, and was not yet practised in the art of flattery so failed to turn his reply into a compliment. Instead he changed the subject.

'How is Archibald?'

'Tethered.'

'What does that mean?'

'Oh dear! I hoped you would teach me how to use a computer, and here you are expecting me to instruct you about horses.'

'Sorry! Where would you like me to start?'

'Would the beginning be a good place, do you think?'

After hearing from Cynthia why there was a horse attached to the railings, Bernard decided to double check on his sobriety by taking a wash and brush-up in the bathroom before settling down for the evening in his favourite arm-chair. When he reached the landing at the top of the first flight of stairs he thought he heard voices coming from the attic. It came back to him what Cynthia had said about Jonathan having a visit from Amy's friend and he listened to hear what they were saying.

What he heard left him wondering if it had been wise to leave two young people of the opposite sex together, alone, in an attic bedroom.

'It's funny, you know,' Daphne was saying, 'but it doesn't look a bit like a mouse!'

Chapter 11

When Amy heard that Daphne had spent the evening with Jonathan in his bedroom she reminded her mother that Bernard had said she could invite Freddie to have lunch with them one day. Cynthia said she knew nothing about such an arrangement and would have to speak to her father first. Bernard explained that the lad had helped him with some inside information while he was working at the supermarket which may have contributed to his losing his job there, so they owed him something in return. Cynthia complained that she ought to have been consulted but in the circumstances agreed that he could come on Sunday.

When Jonathan heard what Amy had achieved he invoked the equal opportunities principle and asked if Daphne could come too. Cynthia said their dining room was not large enough to accommodate six, but Bernard wanted to cultivate his Banner Boy for possible further use should the need arise.

'Why don't you and I eat in the kitchen,' he suggested, 'and let the young ones sit at table in the dining room?'

Cynthia's next worry was what food to prepare for such a meal.

'It's been so long since we entertained young people and I have no idea what they eat these days.' Bernard said they ought to be grateful for whatever she offered them. Amy assured her mother it would be all right if she produced her usual Sunday lunch, only on a larger scale.

After that, Amy lost no time in contacting Freddie, who needed no persuading to accept, but when Jonathan called at *The Brambles* to ask if Daphne would like to join them he was greeted with the shock news that she was in hospital.

It appeared that Daphne had been so impressed by the sight of icons jumping over obstacles while she was in Jonathan's bedroom that on her way home she encouraged Archibald to emulate them. Unfortunately neither she nor the horse had the benefit of an electronic mouse to get them over the ropes dividing part of the field reserved for Archibald from the recently designated car park, and the real obstacle proved too much for either of them.

'I don't know what you and my daughter were up to at your house last night,' said Mrs Trotter, 'or whether she had been drinking something intoxicating, but Daphne fell off her horse and dislocated her shoulder.'

Totally unprepared for this, and embarrassed by the suggestion that he might somehow have been to blame, Jonathan made the mistake of asking what happened to the horse.

'Dear me! I thought it was Daphne you were interested in! But if you really want to know, the horse may have to be destroyed.'

Cynthia wanted to cancel Freddie's visit, or at least postpone it, when she heard that Daphne was in hospital but Bernard said it would be unfair to disappoint the lad, or their daughter, as a result of Daphne's misfortune. Jonathan, who was clearly upset, said there would be no problem about seating arrangements in the dining room because he would take sandwiches and eat them in the hospital gardens after visiting the casualty ward.

Freddie arrived at the Talbots' for lunch on Sunday with a large bunch of flowers but was unsure whether to give them to Amy or her mother. Bernard only added to his discomfort by saying he really ought not to have bothered because it was their pleasure to thank him for what he had already done on their behalf.

Cynthia realised this was the first time her daughter had brought home a boy friend and it marked a new stage in her growing up. Bernard saw it differently. He wanted to encourage a relationship which promised further support for his campaign against the supermarket. Neither parent had thought to ask Amy what her feelings were towards Freddie and even had they done so it is doubtful if they would have taken them seriously.

Over lunch they chatted cheerfully, trying to avoid too many personal questions about Freddie's background, or reminiscences about Amy's childhood, until Bernard found the opportunity to talk about the shop.

'It's going to get more difficult,' he said sombrely, 'to keep this shop open if we can't stand up to the opposition from that place where you and Amy used to work. The day may come,' he said, 'when there won't be a shop left in the village unless we can do something about it soon.'

'You've done your best, dear,' said Mrs Talbot, bravely supporting her husband. 'It won't be your fault if that happens.'

'I'm sure Mr Talbot is right,' said Freddie, 'but I don't suppose you'll ever have the resources to beat the supermarket at their own game. The only way I think you'll stop people using them is to make people want to stay at home and shop in the village!'

'Ah!' said Bernard. 'There's the rub. How do we do that?'

'I think the day will come,' ventured their guest, 'when we'll be able to order all the goods we want by telephone.'

That was an idea Bernard had never considered and he wondered how it would help them in the *General Stores*. Freddie could see a look of disbelief in Bernard's eyes and changed the subject.

'Will there be a village fete again this year?' he asked. 'If there is, I'll get the boys to carry banners with a new slogan if you can think of one.'

'I daresay I could do that, lad! In fact I've got one already. What's more, it fits in with your idea about making people want to stay at home. It's there on the side of our delivery van. It says : LET'S KEEP IT IN THE VILLAGE.'

Freddie said he had seen that message on the van but thought it was a plea to stop it being stolen.

From Bernard's point of view, it was a good lunch, and Freddie thought so too. Amy had the feeling her father had taken Freddie over as his guest, but she didn't mind because it meant he was now a friend of the family. Cynthia was just relieved that no-one had noticed she forgot to salt the potatoes.

Jonathan, meanwhile, had made his first visit to a hospital since he was carried there as a baby to be introduced to Amy on her arrival into the world. He was then too small to remember anything about it but the sight of Daphne sitting up in bed with her arm in a sling would have resembled that of his mother with a babe in her arms.

'Hallo,' he said lamely, trying not to look too closely at her hospital gown.

'Have you come to ask me about the horse?'

'Oh dear, your mother told you, did she?'

'Yes, and she thinks we'd been drinking.'

'What did you tell her we'd been doing?'

'Why, had we been doing anything we shouldn't have?'

'I don't think so!'

Daphne laughed.

'I don't suppose you would have noticed if we had!'

'I wanted to bring you a present, but didn't know what would be suitable. So I brought you this.'

He handed her a peach.

'Oh, how nice. I wonder what made you think of that?'

Maybe it was conceit that made Daphne think of that response, but it pleased Jonathan to know his gift had been appreciated. They passed the next few minutes in awkward silence while Daphne wondered whether she ought to eat the peach or divide it in two and share it. Jonathan watched her fondling the fruit and imagined that one day she might do the same to him. Bashfully, he explained that she was to have been invited to lunch at the *General Stores* and that Amy was there now with her friend, called Freddie, who she met at the supermarket. Daphne said she knew Freddie because he sat next to her at school and said Jonathan ought to warn his sister never to trust him on a dark night. Jonathan looked surprised and said his sister was not allowed out at night, whether it was dark or otherwise. Daphne took hold of his hand and smiled sweetly at him.

'I think, when I get out of here, it will be my turn to teach you a few things you won't find on a computer.'

That evening, in the bar of the *Perch and Parrot*, Freddie was telling his friends about Bernard's slogan.

'He's planning a new campaign to keep the village shops open,' he told them. Then he added: 'I think we ought to help him, don't you?'

'What's in it for us?' asked Gerald.

Billy also lacked enthusiasm. 'I don't fancy carrying another load of banners round the village, if that's what you mean,' he said. 'Can't we do something different this year?'

Mathew, who was a deep thinker, but rarely said much in case it sounded silly, asked if there was really anything in the village worth keeping.

Freddie was about to say 'that was a silly thing to say' when he realised it was a serious question deserving of an answer. Amy's father, he knew, wanted to keep open the *General Stores* because he owned it and lived there, but there was nothing architecturally or historically special about it. In fact, as far as he could see, there was nowhere in the village that had any intrinsic merit. The butcher and baker lived and worked in unpretentious houses; the *Perch and Parrot* had none of the appeal of an old coaching inn; the blacksmith's forge had lost its anvil and was now a shapeless and greasy garage for motor cars. The church, which had known better days and larger congregations, was in need of repair, and only *The Willows*, where the village fete was held, had any interesting features. Reluctantly he came to the conclusion there really weren't any parts of the village worth keeping, but he felt bound to defend it.

'It's where we grew up,' he said, ' and where our homes are, so I wouldn't like to see it fade away. I do agree, though, with what Mr Talbot is saying. If people who live here go on shopping outside the village there soon won't be any shops left in the village. When that happens people either won't want to live here, or won't be able to.'

Mathew began to think about that. If it was a more interesting place he felt sure people would want to live here and there might be enough business for local shops *and* the supermarket.

'In the meantime,' said Lenny, 'if our people keep going into the supermarket to buy goods, couldn't we encourage people from other places to come here to do their shopping?'

'The trouble is our shops can't compete with the supermarket.'

'Which is where we came in!'

'No, that's why our people go out.'

'Hold on! Where is all this getting us?'

'Back on track,' said Freddie. 'What we're saying is if we made the place attractive to visitors, so they came here to see something special, they might stay long enough to buy things in the village.'

Mathew remembered the word he was looking for. It was tourism.

'That's it,' said Freddie. 'We must make Backwater a tourist attraction.'

Bernard was about to set out on his weekly delivery when the telephone rang.

'Mr Talbot, this is Freddie speaking'. (Bernard feared the lad was trying to prove the point he made at lunch about people buying things in future over the telephone.) ' I've been talking to the boys and I think we've come up with an idea to help you.'

'I'm just going out,' said Bernard. 'Could we talk about it this evening?'

Amy was not expecting Freddie when he walked into the shop shortly before closing time.

'Is your father back yet?' he asked her.

'Won't I do?' she pleaded, pouting her lips.

'Later, perhaps, but first I've got something very important to discuss with your father.'

When Cynthia heard him say this she had the romantic notion he was going to ask for their daughter's hand in marriage.

'You'd better take Freddie through into the sitting room,' she whispered to Amy. 'Your father will be home soon.'

In the moments before Bernard returned Amy tried vainly to get Freddie to tell her what it was he wanted to tell her father. All he would say was that he owed it to her father to let him be the first to know.

Amy was now getting the same impression as her mother and was trying to hide her excitement.

'Is it something personal?' she asked.

Freddie shook his head.

'Will you tell me after you've spoken to my father?'

Freddie nodded.

Bernard's appearance in the doorway put a stop to their sparring. He had been hurriedly briefed by Cynthia and before he would let Freddie say what it was he had come about he insisted that Amy should fetch them some glasses and a bottle of wine. This confirmed Amy's suspicion that they wanted to talk about her while she was out of the room. Freddie had no idea he was being misunderstood and kept up a commentary on the weather while waiting for her to return.

'Now then,' said Bernard, when she got back, 'what was it you wanted to tell me on the telephone this morning?'

Freddie gave his account of the discussion which took place in the *Perch and Parrot* the previous night and then made tracks for the door.

'Well, that's about it,' he said. 'I daresay you'll want to think it over.'

'Woa, come back,' said Bernard. 'I've made up my mind already. What you've been saying is absolutely right. The village hasn't got much to commend itself at present, which is why I left it when I were your age. But now I'm back I like it a lot and don't mean to see it decline any further.'

Bernard crossed the room and put his hand on Freddie's shoulder.

'This calls for another drink.'

He then turned to Amy and asked her to refill their glasses.

'You'd better take one in for your mother. And while you're there tell her she can put her imagination to better use when she hears what Freddie has really been saying.'

Amy glared at her father and spilled wine deliberately over his shoes while she was filling her mother's glass. She then handed the bottle to Freddie and flounced out of the room. Bernard resumed his response to Freddie, who was wondering what he had done to upset Amy.

'I suppose,' said Bernard, 'the village must have been a busier place when they built that church and the big house where Mr Thurrock lives. It's a great idea of yours to find ways of making it interesting and attractive again.'

Freddie asked if they should start at once.

'I think we'd better go and consult a few people first,' said Bernard, 'because we may need their help. People like Mr Thurrock, and your old school-master, Mr Formby.'

The chairman of the parish council was surprised to see Bernard at *The Willows* accompanied by someone he recognised as a Banner Boy.

'It's a bit early to talk about the fete, isn't it?' he said.

'We've come to ask your support for an even bigger project,' said Bernard, enigmatically.

'I suppose that means you want me to call another Extraordinary Meeting of the Parish?'

'Well, not yet,' said Bernard, who went on to explain what he wanted, and why he had brought Freddie with him.

Mr Thurrock listened impatiently until Bernard outlined the part which he was expected to play.

'You mean you want me to *invent* some sort of history that will make the place notorious!'

'Not necessarily. Shall we say, *discover,* or perhaps, *reveal.*'

The chairman thought for a moment, as the idea of notoriety began to appeal.

'Would it be true to say you'd like me to *dig up* something from the past?'

Bernard knew then that their mission had succeeded.

Chapter 12

Mr Formby was preparing to go home when Bernard and Freddie were shown into his office. It had been a bad day for the headmaster. One of his boys had been injured in the playground trying to climb over a wall; the art teacher had slipped on a wet floor and knocked herself out on an easel and a disgruntled parent had accused him of humiliating her daughter by standing her in front of the class when she was wearing a dirty uniform.

Unaware of these vicissitudes, Bernard announced that they had come to seek his support for a new campaign to stop people leaving the village.

'What on earth are you planning to do? Will it be barricades this time instead of banners?'

Freddie was familiar with his headmaster's sarcasm and looked uncomfortable. He felt, as he had often done at school, that he was being accused of some misdemeanour, so he owned up to suggesting there was a need to create a new image for the village.

'You'd better not let the vicar hear you say that, young man! He says God created the world and he won't like the idea of you criticising it.'

Bernard went quickly to the rescue.

'Don't be hard on the lad. He wants to defend us against what I've been calling a drift to oblivion. Once everyone buys from the supermarket there won't be a shop left in the village.'

'Well I don't see what I can do to help. It's difficult enough for me to keep children out of mischief. I can't reshape the shopping habits of their parents!'

'Ah,' said Bernard, 'but we were only thinking of you acting for us in an advisory capacity.'

'Like how to make them public spirited? Perhaps you ought to see the vicar after all!'

'No,' said Bernard, 'but, as a teacher of history, we thought you might know what would once have been popular pastimes in the village, so we could recreate them.'

'Like public executions, and punishment in the stocks, you mean?'

Bernard gasped at the idea. 'We had in mind something more cultural, like stripping the maypole and morris dancing. Something to bring back a bit of colour to the village.'

'They're more likely to bring colour to your cheeks these days. If it's that kind of entertainment you want I suggest you form a pop group, or call in the gypsies!'

Bernard was disappointed and asked how the headmaster would feel if half his pupils decamped to another school outside the district.

'I doubt if another school would take them. If it were the half I have trouble with they certainly wouldn't!'

Bernard realised it was a poor analogy, and could see that this mission had failed. On his way back to the *General Stores* he began to wonder if the headmaster was in touch with the world outside his classroom. Looking sadly at Freddie for corroboration he said: 'I bet he never does the shopping!'

That evening Robert Formby asked his wife where she bought the food they were eating. The question was instantly interpreted as a criticism.

'Why what's wrong with it?'

'Nothing dear. I just wondered where you do the shopping.'

Mrs Formby was not accustomed to cross examination, and demanded an explanation. Her husband's account of his interview with Bernard led to her disclosure that she had been shopping at the supermarket ever since it opened. Where did he think she got the salmon he was now eating? She hadn't fished for it, she assured him!

'Don't you ever shop in the village?' he asked her.

'There isn't a fishmonger in the village. Only a fish and chip shop, and that doesn't open until the evening.'

'What about meat, then? There is a butcher in the village.'

'Robert, if you'd rather have meat, why don't you say so. I thought you'd like fish for a change.'

It had already been a difficult day for the headmaster and it was now getting worse.

'I only asked because there seems to be some doubt about how long we can keep shops open in the village now there's a supermarket in the neighbourhood. But, of course, if you don't use the village shops anyway it won't matter to us, will it, if they disappear?'

Put like that, Mrs Formby felt accused.

'Oh, but I wouldn't like that to happen. I'm sure there will always be some people who'd rather buy in the village.' She thought for a moment, and saw her husband look away. 'I suppose, if they haven't got a car they won't be able to get to the supermarket.' Her husband nodded. As an afterthought she added 'Besides, they do rather encourage you to spend more in a supermarket than you would in the village.'

Robert Formby stopped short of asking if she was spending more than she need by going there. Instead he remarked that he could see the time coming when there wouldn't be enough money being spent locally to make it worth running a shop in the village.

'I suppose,' he sighed, 'the time might come when they won't need a school here either.'

The debate continued after their meal and well into the night. By morning Mrs Formby had resolved to buy only occasionally from the supermarket, and the headmaster had decided to look more kindly at Bernard's plan to keep people shopping in the village.

Bernard, meantime, had decided to take the headmaster's advice and call on the Reverend Lovelock. Before doing so he divested himself of Freddie because he feared the vicar might be less supportive in the presence of a young man he knew only as a Banner Boy. He was not prepared for the abrupt reception.

'Ah,' said the vicar, 'come in. I have been meaning to ask you to reconsider your decision to open your shop on Sundays.'

Bernard took a deep breath and reminded the vicar that *his* shop had always been open on a Sunday.

'I never considered that was a threat to the *General Stores*,' he said, 'so why do you think I might be taking people away from the church now? Have you really noticed any falling off in your congregation since I started opening on Sundays?'

Aware that he was losing the argument, Vernon Lovelock allowed himself to smile.

'Well, I have observed one or two of my parishioners falling off during the sermon.'

'No, vicar, that was not what I meant, but I thought you might have noticed fewer of our village folk going to church now that the supermarket has opened.'

'I fear so,' said the vicar. 'But there are other distractions.'

Bernard did not wait to hear them. He was keen to retain the initiative.

'If the congregation gets smaller there'll be less in the collection, until one day your plate will be empty.'

'Oh dear me, yes,' said the vicar, shaking his head dramatically, 'but, of course, we mustn't dwell on mercenary considerations. What matters is the faith.'

'Indeed,' said Bernard, driving home his message, 'but my question to you is how much faith do you have in the future of our village?'

Vernon Lovelock was confused. His silence allowed Bernard to continue.

'The truth is, Vernon,' he said, choosing this moment to address him informally, 'we are in real danger of losing our local population and I am looking for ways of encouraging people to stay here, in the village.'

Never before had the vicar looked upon Bernard as a saviour. A campaigner, yes, for he knew about his banners and petitions, but this sounded more like the call of a missionary.

'I'll tell you what we have in mind,' said Bernard. He used the plural to increase the impact. 'We want Backwater to be a village where people can feel they have a history to be proud of. Unfortunately, there isn't much about the place nowadays which they can recognise as notable or historic. So what I would like you to do is look through your parish records to see if anyone important ever lived here, or if anything remarkable happened in the past that would make us memorable.'

A long silence followed. Vernon wasn't sure that he knew where to look for the parish records. Perhaps he would consult the bishop. Was it possible that the vicarage concealed a mystery that would make it famous? Might it affect his stipend if he helped bring notoriety to the village?

Bernard sensed the need for a little persuasion.

'There is a village in Derbyshire,' he said, 'where people were once dying of the plague. To prevent the infection spreading, the vicar stopped everyone from going out or coming in. You could go down to posterity as the vicar who stopped his villagers leaving because he gave them back their heritage.'

On his way home, after sharing a bottle of ginger wine with the vicar, Bernard bumped into Mr Barlow.

'Look where you're going, man! Oh, I'm sorry. It's you, Bernard.'

'Forgive me for staggering,' said Bernard, 'but I have just had a most encouraging meeting with the vicar.'

'Don't tell me he's agreed to shorten his sermons on Sundays!'

'Afraid I wouldn't know about that, but he's agreed to search the parish records and try to dig up a bit of local history.'

Mr Barlow thought for a moment.

'Funny you should say that,' he said, 'but our parish chairman has just spent the day digging up parts of his garden. He said he was looking for bones, or pottery, but he doesn't keep a dog, and he's never shown much interest in archaeology.'

Bernard guessed what he was doing, and told Mr Barlow he was probably trying to find something memorable to add lustre to the village.

'Perhaps you'd like to join in the hunt,' he suggested. 'We're looking for ways of bringing back the past, so as to make the future more interesting.'

Mr Barlow concluded that the wine had gone to his head, and walked on.

Bernard arrived home to find Jonathan had heard from Daphne that Archibald, her horse, had died. His retort was uncharacteristic but in keeping with Mr Barlow's diagnosis.

'I hope that doesn't mean we'll have horse-meat for lunch on Sunday.'

Jonathan ignored the remark and said Daphne was very upset.

'She wants it buried in the field, close to where it fell.'

Bernard suddenly took an interest.

'I don't know who she'll get to dig a grave deep enough to bury a horse,' he said, 'but if she needs any help I may be able to oblige.'

This took Cynthia by surprise. Bernard had never shown much interest in gardening and the thought of him labouring with a spade did not ring true. Amy looked equally disturbed.

'It's very good of you to offer, Dad, but I daresay Mr Trotter will know someone who deals with horses.'

'Live ones, yes, I'm sure,' said Bernard, 'but dead ones I doubt! Don't get me wrong, I wasn't offering to do the digging myself, but I have just made friends with someone who, you might say, is a regular employer of grave-diggers.'

Cynthia was now alarmed, but before she could ask her husband where he had been and what he had been drinking, he said he had just come back from the vicarage where he had given the vicar an idea that would endear him forever to his congregation.

'In return I'm sure I can get him to offer Old Butch the services of his professional grave diggers.'

What he did not explain to Cynthia was that a hole in the butcher's field large enough to bury a horse would improve the chance of making a discovery supporting his vision that the village had an interesting past.

To Bernard's chagrin, however, when he put his proposal to the butcher, George Trotter said he was not at all inclined to finance his daughter's extravagant burial suggestion.

'I've told her,' he said, 'I shall arrange for the carcass to be disposed of at a knacker's yard.

Bernard had to resort to artfulness to persuade his friend to change his mind.

'They'd have to dig deep to inter an animal that size, and you never know what they might find in your field. Folk have been known to uncover hoards of old coins worth thousands of pounds in today's currency. Or, you might be lucky and strike oil!'

Butch looked doubtful and shook his head.

'More likely they'll find mud and water!'

But when Bernard told him the parish chairman was already digging at *The Willows* he showed more interest.

'Well, p'raps I wouldn't mind having a look beneath *The Brambles*, but we'd better not let Daphne know or she'll say we're insensitive.'

They chuckled over the arrangement and agreed that as joint beneficiaries of the car parking facility they would request the vicar to employ his grave-diggers at their expense.

The commission was duly carried out, but it was not coins they found at the bottom of the pit, or oil, or water, but the fossil remains of a very large animal.

Chapter 13

The sight of bones at the bottom of the pit they were digging took the four men with shovels completely by surprise. They were nowhere near the church and had no reason to believe a graveyard ever existed in that part of the village. One of the diggers suggested they had struck the roots of a tree, but closer inspection confirmed their fears that what they were looking at was bones. Shovels were dropped and shivers ran down their backs. Leader of the party was despatched to fetch the vicar.

'Oughtn't we to call the police?' said the second in command.

'How do we do that?' asked the third man. 'You 'on't find a constable in these parts.'

'Let's fill the hole in and dig somewhere else,' said the last of the diggers.

When the vicar arrived he was no more decisive about what action they should take, but gave it as his opinion that since the hole was so deep and the bones lay at the bottom of it they must have been buried a long time ago.

'No-one from the village has been buried outside the churchyard since I became vicar,' he assured them. 'Perhaps we ought to ask the bishop.'

It was then that George Trotter appeared, having noticed the comings and goings from his shop window. On hearing what was causing the fuss he went back to the house and telephoned the constabulary in a neighbouring village.

An hour later two detectives arrived in a police car and began taking statements from George Trotter, the vicar and each of the gravediggers.

'You'll not be moving the body before the bishop sees it, I hope,' said the vicar. 'He may know if it has been blessed or not.'

A detective said that any examination would have to be conducted by a qualified pathologist.

'And we'll need to inform the coroner,' added his companion.

'How long will all that take?' asked Butch who was wondering what would happen in the meantime to the horse.

'I expect the pathologist can be here by the morning,' said the senior detective. 'Meantime we'd better put a cordon round the pit and go home for the night.'

Daphne was out of hospital but *hors de combat*. Throughout the day she heard reports of what was happening in the field from her mother and father but at night her imagination took over and she struggled to envisage how those bones got into the ground over which she used to ride her horse. In her mind she pictured a gruesome murder being committed by bloodstained men and their victim's body carried through the undergrowth to be buried in the dead of night. Either that or some ritual of human sacrifice enacted in the past when Backwater was a mere settlement of pagan worshippers. By morning her mother found her clutching the pillow, her bedclothes wrapped tightly round a trembling body.

Soon after she woke, a pathologist called at the house and was directed to the field opposite where he carried out a brief inspection and announced that the bones at the bottom of the pit were not human.

'So what happens now?' asked Mrs Trotter.

The answer was that they had sent for an anthropologist.

Meanwhile, rumour was spreading through the village that something nasty had been found in a field near *The Brambles*. Local inhabitants kept well clear of the site, but strangers who picked up the gossip made straight for the field and stared into the hole.

About midday, a Dr Chalmers arrived in a jeep, dressed as if prepared for a safari, slid down into the pit, and declared that the bones were probably from a prehistoric animal. After taking photographs from different angles, he placed one of the bones in a plastic bag and took it back to his university for closer examination.

The problem, which now confronted the butcher, and more especially his daughter, was where to find another place to bury the horse. Daphne spoke to Amy when she called to see her that evening, and Amy told her father who thought of the excavations taking place at *The Willows*. Anxious to help the butcher resolve his dilemma, Bernard set off to see Mr Thurrock and asked him if any of the holes being dug in his garden were large enough to accommodate a horse.

'Been losing at the races, have you?' was the response.

Unprepared for such joviality, Bernard explained why they could no longer bury the horse where they intended. When the parish chairman learned what had been found in a pit on the butcher's field his humour changed and he cursed the gardener for not digging deeper at *The Willows*. The prospect of finding fossils in his own garden was enough to ensure access to the entire estate.

'Come in,' he said 'and dig as deep as you like. But if you find any bones here you'll have to get that horse cremated. Or else eat it!'

The vicar's gravediggers were not too keen about another commission so soon after the one they had just aborted. Moreover, they were unaccustomed to digging graves among bushes in a private garden. However, encouraged by the offer of a bonus if they uncovered the remains of any more prehistoric animals, they excavated enough soil to bury a couple of elephants. By nightfall the chairman was convinced that if any such creatures did inhabit his property in the past none of them had perished there.

Mr Thurrock was disappointed but gave future generations the opportunity to succeed where he had failed by allowing the butcher to fill one of the holes with Daphne's horse.

Butch's next problem was what to do with the bones of an animal that were now being measured and photographed in full view of the shop where he sold meat for human consumption. He was not alone in wanting them taken away, for the anthropologist wanted them all to be removed to his laboratory for further study, and the curator of a nearby museum wanted to exhibit them in a showcase with other prehistoric remains from the district. Bernard, however, saw the opportunity to capitalise on the event and urged Mr Thurrock to help keep the skeleton in the village.

As chairman of their council, Mr Thurrock said he ought to allow parishioners a voice on where the remains should rest, but Bernard warned him that another Extraordinary Meeting might produce an unwelcome result.

'I daresay many people in the village would treat those bones just like they do with what's left on their plates after dinner on Sunday. But those bones in old Butch's field are precious because they can help us achieve what we're after and put this village back on the map. Don't you see? When the news gets out, people will come for miles to look at them. Those bones have been here longer than anything else in the village, and they may even be of national importance.'

Mr Thurrock gave an impression of being thoughtful.

'Perhaps we ought to consult Mr Formby. He may have room to store the skeleton in a school cupboard.'

Bernard saw the joke but said he thought a showcase in the *Perch and Parrot*, alongside the framed fish and stuffed bird, might be a better place to display it.

So, Bernard went to see the publican and Mr Thurrock called upon the schoolmaster.

Inside the *Perch and Parrot* Bernard found a group of local villagers gathered round a stranger who was asking them what they knew about the discovery of animal remains in the field opposite the butcher.

'I shouldn't believe all you hear,' said one of the regulars renowned for his generous contributions to the supply of rumours, 'but if there were any bones in that pit they're as likely to be ones what Old Butch throwed there himself.'

'Aye,' said another, picking up the drift, 'but I reckon they looked more likely to have come from a horse than a heifer!'

Bernard recognised the stranger as a reporter from *The Scribe*, and was aghast at the way in which his friend was being slandered. He was about to intervene and put the record straight, when it occurred to him that the real story would have less reader appeal than a mystery about the origin of a prehistoric monster. So he left it at that. He also left without asking the publican if he would give a permanent resting place to the bones when the scientists had finished with them.

Next morning, *The Scribe* carried the news that an anthropologist had described the bones in Butch's field as possibly those of a dinosaur. It also said that an archaeologist was planning to explore the site for further evidence. There was a picture of *The Brambles* and a snapshot of scientists at work in the field opposite.

The excitement of seeing his shop on the front page of a newspaper assuaged George Trotter's anger at the implication of dumping. On the premise that any publicity was better than none he pasted a copy of the newspaper in his window for all his customers to see. When Daphne was shown the paper she was not amused and said they should have buried her horse on top of the dinosaur and not disturbed the bones. That way, she said, Archibald would have had the dignity of sharing a tomb with a distinguished antecedent.

Later that day, the other Archibald, Archibald Thurrock, had a difficult meeting when he called on the schoolmaster. Robert Formby was again smarting from the whiplash of a disgruntled parent's tongue, and regarded the request to accommodate a dinosaur skeleton as the straw which broke the camel's back.

'If you had asked me to stuff Mrs Whitaker's skeleton in a school cupboard I would have gladly obliged, but the idea of hoarding a prehistoric monster on the premises when I have so many live monsters to deal with in this establishment fills me with horror. I'm sorry, Archie, but the answer is no.'

Surprised by the familiarity, Archie Thurrock smiled and accepted the response as final. He was reminded of how he had once felt, in similar surroundings, when he failed an examination, but as he passed through the school gate on his way out he derived some comfort from knowing how well he had done since, even without a certificate. Comparing notes with Bernard the following morning he confessed that it might have been better if they had gone to the *Perch and Parrot* together and forgotten about the schoolmaster. Then they could have drowned their sorrows and given the reporter something to write home about.

The story which did appear in *The Scribe* carried the headline STRAIGHT FROM THE HORSE'S MOUTH and was read by the editor of a local radio station who sent his own reporter with a tape recorder to follow it up.

Giles Faversham reached the butcher's field as Amy was delivering a tray of drinks to the anthropologist and an archaeologist who had just arrived on site. Mistaking Amy for a waitress, he asked if she would bring two more drinks for himself and his mate with the tape recorder.

'The drinks,' said Amy, 'were a gift from my father, but you can buy some for yourselves if you follow me back to the *General Stores.*'

The reporter apologised and said he had come from *Radio Rustic* to get some background on the story published in the local newspaper. He needed no persuasion to follow Amy back to the shop. On the way she told him the story of how Daphne had fallen off her horse ... which had since died from its injury ... and was to have been buried in the field ... until they unearthed the remains of a dinosaur.

'If it hadn't been for Daphne,' Amy added, 'they would never have discovered such a treasure.'

The reporter felt the same way about Amy, but said he would like to meet Daphne.

'I'll take you to my house first to get your drinks,' said Amy, 'then I'll ask my brother to take you to her. He's been going out with her recently, so I'm sure he'll be pleased to take you. She lives at *The Brambles* right opposite the field where they're digging.'

Fascinated by Amy's chatter, Giles was in no hurry to be handed over to her brother, and Amy, who had her own agenda, was in no hurry to let go of the reporter.

Oblivious to the fact that she was being recorded, Amy went on to say that when people in the village heard they were digging out bones, from what was meant to be a grave for Daphne's horse, someone suggested Daphne's father had been dumping meat there that he couldn't sell in the shop.

Giles glanced at his companion to make sure he was still switched on.

When they reached the *General Stores* Jonathan was not there, so Amy sold the reporters some cans of drink and took them to *The Brambles* herself. There they were introduced to Mr Trotter and recorded his version of the story.

'Is it true?' asked Giles. 'Did you really bury bones in that field?'

Old Butch took hold of the microphone and waved it in the air.

'If I ever meet up with whoever started that story I'll put *his* bones down there!'

Before leaving the village the reporters crossed the field and interviewed the scientists but, back in the studio, they found the editor was more interested in what he called the human story as told by Amy and George Trotter.

'Go back tomorrow,' said the editor, 'and get more from that girl in the shop. She sounds exciting.'

Giles agreed, but thought 'excitable' was a better epithet.

Cynthia was in the shop when he got there next morning and, thinking he had come to buy more of the drinks which Amy sold him the previous day, she was surprised to be told he had come to interview her daughter.

'Oh dear, you're not going to ask her to repeat that story about how bones got into the butcher's field, are you? I do hope not!'

Giles said his editor wanted him to get Amy to talk about village life 'as seen through the eyes of a young person'.

Amy heard this as she came into the shop and said she would be glad to oblige, so long as she could say what she liked and not be censored.

Her mother feared the worst, but need not have worried.

Amy's broadcast was heralded by the local radio station as promising a revelation of youth's attitude to rural life, and many people in the village tuned in to hear if she would tell them anything they did not know already. In the event her views turned out to be less surprising than her mother expected, but more audacious than her editor imagined.

She began with a few short yeses and nos to some straightforward questions.

'Yes,' she did miss the wide streets and bright lights of a big city.

'No,' she did not want to go back there to live.

'Yes,' it did take a long time to feel at home with her classmates at school.

'No,' they were not a rough and unruly lot!

'I suppose,' she said, 'they were just as surprised to find me like them as I was to find them like me.'

There were no more monosyllabic replies. From then on Amy chatted about her father's business and the way her friends had helped him campaign against the supermarket.

'I wonder,' she said, 'if all of you who live in this lovely village of Backwater realise the struggle my parents are having to keep open the *General Stores* now that a supermarket has taken away so many of their customers.'

She confessed to her own disloyalty of going to work there instead of in her family's shop, but said she took home some useful tips about how the place was run before they gave her the sack.

'Oh, why were you sacked?' she was asked.

'Because the manager found out where I lived and thought I was trying to sabotage his business.'

'Were you?'

'No.'

'You mean you were dismissed when they discovered your father was a competitor?'

Amy said it showed how ruthless a big business could be.

'It may not be long before there won't be any shops left in the village.' Staring fiercely into the microphone, she added, 'Then those of you who are older than my Mum or Dad will have to find new ways to do your shopping. Either that, or you'll have to live somewhere else.'

Sensing she might have exceeded her interviewer's remit, she concluded, enigmatically: 'Some of my young friends are planning to make the village more interesting in future. I do hope they succeed because there are still lots of us who wouldn't want to live anywhere else.'

Amy's interview was the topic of conversation throughout the village. Bernard was delighted, and said he could not have put the case better himself.

The radio station received more calls of congratulation than those of protest, and considered the broadcast a great success. A few days later Amy received a letter offering her a permanent job as a radio commentator.

Chapter 14

Dr Chalmers, the anthropologist who was reported to have identified the bones as those of a dinosaur, was attached to a university which had until recently been a polytechnic. He was, therefore, keen to capitalise on the discovery by establishing a high profile research programme which, he hoped, would lead to publication and possibly a professorial appointment. He had not yet unearthed a complete skeleton but envisaged being able to do so and sought permission to resume digging as soon as possible. Meantime, however, he had some unexpected competition to deal with.

The archaeologist who followed him to the site was a young woman he had not seen since they were students together at London University. He recognised her at once as Evelyn Oldfield and their reunion at the bottom of a pit in George Trotter's field had all the ingredients of a clandestine romance. However, the pleasure of finding an old flame alongside the remains of an old reptile soon evaporated. He quickly recognised that any reward for their researches would now have to be shared.

'What brings you to this god-forsaken hole?' he asked her. 'As an archaeologist I thought you would be interested in old civilisations, not old fossils. Aren't we a few million years too early for you on this site?'

'Not necessarily,' she said. 'Early man used sharpened bones as tools and weapons so he might have settled over a site where prehistoric bones were buried.'

'Well, if you're going to settle over my fossils, we'd better dig together. How sharp are your nails?'

Evelyn showed him. They were clearly capable of drawing blood.

After a few more explorative exchanges, they decided to call upon the owner of the field and ask permission to continue excavating in search of other remains. They found the butcher in an uncooperative mood. He said it would interfere with his trade and wanted the hole filled up as soon as possible.

Dr Chalmers pleaded with him, in the interest of science, to let them dig a little longer.

'The more you dig the bigger the hole will get, and the more there'll be to fill in when you've gone!'

Evelyn assured him they would be happy to put the soil back once they had found what they were looking for.

'Suppose you don't find what you're looking for?'

'Oh, but we will,' said Dr Chalmers. 'We can see it's there already. All we need is time to complete the recovery.'

'Good God! You're not thinking of bringing it back to life, I hope!'

That gave them all a good laugh and the two scientists were struggling to think of a new approach when they were joined by Bernard.

'Sorry if I'm interrupting,' he said, 'but would these two good people be the scientists I've heard about? ... I take it you've come to help us discover a bit of our local history?'

Butch was not pleased to prolong the discussion.

'I've just told them all this talk about dead animals in that field opposite my shop is bad for my business.'

'Ah, but in the long run,' said Bernard, 'it could be good for trade all over the village if news gets out that we're sitting on a goldmine of prehistoric relics.'

Anthropologist looked at archaeologist and nodded affirmation.

In spite of his reluctance Butch was eventually persuaded to allow work to continue, and the two scientists walked back across the field: one to look for fossils and the other for signs of previous habitation.

In the meantime, Vernon Lovelock, the vicar, was taking a rare stroll among the tombstones in his graveyard. He had taken to heart what Bertrand said about his dwindling congregation, and looked up what the vicar of Eyam had done at the time of the plague. It was all very well, he thought, to be judged by history as famous for doing something that just happened to be opportune, but he failed to see what he could do to stop people getting their groceries and other commodities from a neighbouring supermarket! However, if Bertrand was right and some of his parishioners had ancestors who were distinguished or prosperous perhaps that would help to restore the village to its former glory. He was trying to work out how it would help when he tripped over a sunken tomb and awoke from his reverie.

Looking around the churchyard, he realised how overgrown it had become, and how sad it was that so many graves were now neglected or obscured. Headstones had slipped from the vertical, and inscriptions were scarcely readable. He could understand what Bernard meant about the village being run down and in need of revival. Yet, as he searched for the names of those who were buried there he found few that reminded him of anyone now living. There were epitaphs describing cause of death or piety of the interred, but none that indicated fame or fortune.

The Reverend Lovelock feared he would fail to provide the evidence which Bernard hoped for. Then, as he returned to the vicarage, he had one last revelation. Judging by the size and quality of some of the headstones, and the extravagance of lettering carved on them, it was clear that people in the village had once enjoyed a better standard of living than they did now. That at least would suggest Backwater had not always been what its name implied.

While Vernon Lovelock was in the churchyard studying the record of its inhabitants for a measure of their past attainments, Robert Formby was in a classroom at the village school attempting to teach a future generation some fundamental facts that might help *them* become successful.

Originally built to cater for village children of all ages, the school was now exclusively used for juniors, many of whom lived in neighbouring villages. 'Mr Formby', as he was properly known to the children, had been surprised when one of them asked if it was true that a dinosaur had been found in a field near the butchers. He was even more surprised when he realised that the children imagined the creature was still alive, roaming the countryside where they lived. It did not take him long to correct that impression but it made him think perhaps he had been wrong to dismiss Bernard's suggestion of showing some interest in Backwater's past.

Applying the art of delegation, Mr Formby called upon his deputy teacher, Colin Johnson, to find out what was known locally about the village history.

'Get the children to ask their parents and grandparents what they remember about the days when they were kids. Tell them to write an essay on the subject. Like as not some of the parents will write it for them!'

Mr Johnson did as instructed, and rued the day.

As predicted, one boy described working conditions and rates of pay in such detail that the essay read as if it had been dictated by his father. Another essay gave a graphic account of men getting drunk and beating up their wives, which had the hallmark of a much abused mother. Among the female contributions was one from a girl who described the night her mother was dancing in the village hall when the lights went out. This, she said, was when her father came on the scene. Top prize for candour went to the girl who wrote that her grandmother admitted to a frolic in the harvest field which ended in a shotgun marriage to her grandfather.

None of this was likely to please Bernard. He had hoped to learn how some of the games and rituals had been performed in days past so they could be revived to attract visitors and bring new business to the village. Sadly, Mr Johnson had forgotten to ask for this kind of information. Even before any of the essays were read, Mrs Whitaker had been in the head's study asking what he meant by encouraging the children to pry into their parent's backgrounds and personal affairs. Consequently, Mr Johnson was forbidden to repair his omission by repeating the exercise.

At *The Willows*, Archie Thurrock had been looking wistfully at all the holes dug in his garden and he regretted the lack of evidence that anything of interest had ever been buried there. Musing over Bernard's wish to stop people shopping in the supermarket, he facetiously thought of linking up the holes and creating a moat around the village. He felt aggrieved and envious, and walked over to *The Brambles* to see what it was that had died there instead of at *The Willows*.

When he reached the butcher's field he was surprised to find a young female at the bottom of the pit scraping away at the soil with what looked like a surgical instrument.

'I say!' he called to her. 'Are you the … a-pologist?'

'Who are you?' asked Evelyn.

'I'm the parish chairman, and you haven't answered my question.'

Evelyn climbed out of the hole to meet her inquisitor.

'Sorry!' she spluttered. 'No, I'm not what you thought I was. I'm an archaeologist. Dr Chalmers is the anthropologist and he's taken the bones to his lab for analysis. I'm here looking for signs of ancient life.'

The expression on Archie's face might have led her to think she need look no further.

'Would you mind repeating that?' he gasped.

When she did, he confessed he thought she had said the doctor had taken the bones to his lavatory for a something-or-other. Her chuckle was infectious and it encouraged him to ask more about the excavation.

By the time he got to the end of his questioning, Mr Thurrock was full of admiration for Miss Oldfield's enthusiasm.

'Perhaps you'd like to look for some signs of ancient life in my garden,' he suggested.

'I'd love to,' she replied.

'Then you must come to *The Willows* tomorrow. And bring your scalpel with you!'

But before then she had an unexpected date with a reporter from *Radio Rustic*.

Soon after joining the staff of the local radio station Amy had been called into the office of the station controller.

'I liked the way you spoke when you were interviewed,' he told her. 'Now we must see how well you can interview others. Go down to the field where they're still digging and get that archaeologist to tell you what she's found – or hopes to find.'

Amy was taken aback. She had not expected to be thrown in so soon. And at the deep end!

'Just stick this recorder in your handbag and hold the microphone where you can both speak into it. Preferably not at the same time, of course! And don't worry. If you make a mess of it we'll treat it as training and throw it away. On the other hand if it's good we'll use it. Now, off you go and enjoy yourself.'

Amy felt sick, but set off to meet Miss Oldfield.

She called first at *The Brambles* for a chat with Daphne who was still recovering from her injury.

Daphne was excited to hear that Amy was about to interview a scientist.

'What sort of questions will you ask her?'

Amy said she didn't know and rather wished she had paid more attention to the subject when she was at school.

'You'll be all right,' said Daphne. 'You were always better than me at science.'

'The trouble is,' said Amy, 'it'll be like talking to someone in a foreign language. I may think of questions to ask, but if I can't understand the answers I shan't know what to say next.'

Daphne tried to put her mind at rest.

'How many of your listeners will know any more than you do? So why not ask whatever comes into your head and let the answers explain themselves.'

That sounded comforting, but as she was crossing the field Amy thought perhaps science was not the only subject her friend was not so good at.

When she reached the pit where Evelyn was standing Amy realised it was considerably larger than she expected. Instead of seeing a grave that was deep and wide enough to hold a coffin, what she saw was a steep rectangular cutting like the foundation for a new house. Staring into it with a trowel in her hand was a woman she guessed must be the archaeologist. Amy approached her boldly, but with butterflies in her stomach.

'I've come to ask you some questions', she said. 'Do you mind?'

Amy looked young enough to be still at school and Evelyn thought she was doing a project for her exams.

'You'd better tell me first what you are studying.'

'I'm not. I'm working. I've been sent by *Radio Rustic* to interview you.'

'Oh dear!' cried Evelyn. 'What do you want to know?'

'I'm supposed to ask you what you are doing here and what you are looking for.'

Evelyn explained that as an archaeologist she was looking for evidence that people may have lived in the area a very long time ago.

'Do you ever wish you had lived at some time in the past?' Amy asked her.

'Frequently,' said Evelyn, 'especially when I'm being interviewed.'

'Thanks,' said Amy. 'That's made me wish I could jump into a hole like that one there!'

'Sorry,' said Evelyn. 'Why don't we jump in together and carry on the interview down there.'

They did, and the recorded interview was broadcast later that evening.

While her mother and father were listening to her on the radio, after they closed shop for the day, Amy was in the *Perch and Parrot* listening with Freddie. He was amused by the broadcast and said she would make a natural quizmaster. She was flattered but said she felt guilty about being back at work while he was unemployed.

'Don't worry,' he said, 'I've asked Mr Perryman if he'll give me a job here at the *Perch and Parrot*.'

'What will you do? Roll out the barrels, or throw out the rowdies?'

'Earn some money instead of spending it, I suppose. Maybe I can talk some customers into helping your old man with his crusade.'

Bernard may not have approved of being described in that manner but when Amy told him the news he was pleased to hear Freddie would soon be back at work. He said he would rather see Freddie behind a bar in a public house than behind any other kind of bars. She knew her father was not a regular customer of public houses but fancied he would not object to Freddie seeking support from those who were.

Meanwhile, preposterous thoughts were passing through the mind of Archie Thurrock as he prepared to entertain Evelyn Oldfield at *The Willows*. He knew she was young enough to be his daughter but would she, he wondered, think he had improper intentions by inviting her to his house. Indeed, was his objective as innocent as he wanted her to believe?

Did he believe she would find signs of an old civilisation beneath the soil of his estate, or would she detect a sign that old inclinations had been reawakened? Putting such thoughts to one side, he placed the garden furniture and unpacked a picnic basket so they could sit together and take lunch in the garden.

Evelyn was also having doubts about the wisdom of accepting an invitation from a man who she hardly knew, who was old enough to be her father. If indeed he was the parish chairman he ought at least to be responsible. But was he also above reproach? Come to that, was *she*? It made her blush to think of the speed with which she had responded to his invitation.

OK, so she was old enough to look after herself, but what ought she to wear? *The Willows* sounded like a distinguished residence, so perhaps she should go in a dress, or something more formal than jeans. Yet, surely if she had been asked in a professional capacity she ought to go in working clothes. He did, after all, say 'be sure to bring your scalpel'. Or was that for self-defence?

It rained soon after she arrived at *The Willows*, so she was glad she chose to go in jeans and sweater. Archie was also dressed for the garden, and was showing her round it when the rain started.

'We'd better stand in the summer house,' said Archie, 'or we'll get wet.'

It sounded safer than 'upstairs with the etchings'.

Then Archie changed his mind.

'On second thoughts,' he said, 'perhaps you'd like me to show you round the house, until the rain stops?'

Nervously she followed him indoors. But there were no etchings. The rain continued, but Evelyn failed to notice. She found the house enchanting and her escort charming. They ate their picnic in the kitchen and when the rain stopped they returned to the garden where Evelyn was shown the holes which the gardener had dug.

Before she left, Archie said there was a room in the house for her to stay in if she wished.

Chapter 15

Freddie's job at the *Perch and Parrot* was to clear the tables and wash up the empty glasses, which was something he had never been required to do at home. His previous work experience, dealing with deliveries at the supermarket, equipped him for the task and he tackled it manfully and cheerfully. This pleased the publican who soon encouraged him to learn the art of tapping the barrels and drawing the beer.

When he was serving customers from behind the bar, he amused himself by trying to imagine what they did for a living; when collecting glasses and emptying the ash-trays he listened to their conversations and pretended to be deaf to what he heard.

It was on one such occasion that he passed two people drinking at a corner table and overheard them talking about the excavation on Butch's field. They were evidently arguing about what they might find if they went on digging. The woman, who Freddie later discovered was Evelyn Oldfield, was saying she wanted to extend the dig as far as *The Willows* because she believed she had found evidence of Early Saxon remains in the garden. Her companion, Dr Chalmers, sounded angry, as though he disapproved of her digging at *The Willows*, and was heard to say she hadn't a hope of finding anything of archaeological interest there 'except possibly in the house!' Evelyn's reply was prompt and equally heated.

'You were wrong about the dinosaur and I'll prove you wrong again about *The Willows*.'

Freddie had to move out of earshot and missed the end of the argument, but he grasped the significance of what he had heard and reported it later to Amy. When Amy relayed it to her father, Bernard said he was sorry to hear this because he had been relying upon the dinosaur story to bring visitors to the village, and more customers to the *General Stores*.

'The doctor may have been wrong about whose bones they were, but if they weren't human and didn't belong to a dinosaur, whose were they do you suppose?'

Amy could not answer that, but said she would discuss it in the morning with her producer when she got to the studio.

Bernard begged her not to be hasty.

'It may be a mistake,' he said, 'or he may have discovered something even more interesting. Let's wait 'til he makes an announcement, in case it's a false alarm.'

Amy reminded her father she was now in business as a reporter and what Freddie had told her was a scoop that would delight her employers.

'It's what they call a conflict of interest,' she chuckled, 'and I've just declared it.'

'Well, I declare it's a conflict of loyalties,' said Bernard, 'and you ought to consider the damage you'll do to our business if you break the news prematurely.'

Amy said he was being unreasonable because there was nothing yet to get damaged, except her reputation if the newspapers broke the story first. Cynthia managed to resolve the argument by suggesting Amy should seek another interview with Miss Oldfield and ask her for the latest news about the discovery.

Amy did tell her producer at *Radio Rustic* what Freddie had overheard in the *Perch and Parrot*, and he repeated the advice her mother gave her.

'I think we'd better wait until we have something more definite to go on. Why don't you pay your friend Miss Oldfield another visit and ask her whether she's found anything lately that might be of interest.'

Amy lost no time and made straight for *The Willows*. When the door was opened by the parish chairman she asked if she could speak to Evelyn Oldfield.

'Miss Oldfield doesn't live here, you know. Well, not yet, anyway!'

Amy said she thought she might be working in the garden.

'Young lady, she's not my gardener!'

Amy was spared further embarrassment by the appearance of Evelyn waving to her from the shrubbery.

'Oh, I see,' said the chairman. 'Why didn't you say she was expecting you?'

Evelyn had not been expecting a visitor, or another interview, and was relieved when Amy told her she had just come along to let her know that their interview on Butch's field had been a success. It was a spur of the moment reply, and a trick of the trade which Amy was learning fast.

Unaware of the pretence, Evelyn smiled and led Amy into the garden.

'You know,' she said as they stared into one of the holes, 'when Mr Thurrock showed me where his gardener had been digging I told him I expected to see little piles of earth around the holes. You're quite right, he said, it looked like moles had been having a field day. So he asked the gardener to mix them with the compost.'

Amy asked if anything other than soil had been found in the holes.

'No, but I did find something interesting in the compost.'

'What was it?'

'Pieces of old pottery.'

'How old were they, do you think?'

'I can't be sure yet, but I've sent them away to the museum to be dated. I think they may be Early Saxon.'

Amy wondered how she could be sure it was not a broken flower pot she had unearthed, but Evelyn anticipated the question.

'I'm afraid I haven't found any more yet, so there's nothing I can show you, but I have seen fragments of that kind before and they're certainly not modern.'

'Do you think you *will* find more where they came from?'

'Yes, I do. But the trouble is, I don't really know where they came from.'

Amy looked puzzled.

'You see,' said Evelyn, 'they were near the top of the heap and could have come from any of the holes which the gardener dug.'

'Does that mean you'll have to dig in all those places again?'

'I'm not even sure they came from those holes, because they might have come from the hole the gravediggers dug?'

'But that's been refilled - with Daphne's horse!'

'Which is why I shall continue to work my way through the rest of the compost. However, if I don't find any more there I may seek permission to exhume the horse.'

Amy shuddered.

'Perhaps you'd better come back another time,' said Evelyn, 'when I've got something tangible to show you.'

Unlike such activity at *The Willows*, it had been a quiet day in the butcher's shop and George Trotter was putting back into the refrigerator cuts of meat which had not been sold that day. Business was not as good as it used to be and he wondered how long he could keep going if customers continued to buy their meat elsewhere. For a time he blamed the increasing popularity of vegetarianism, and then the sale of fast foods like pies and pizzas, but slowly he was coming round to Bernard's view that too many people in the village were shopping at the supermarket.

After wiping down the shelves when he had cleared them of meat he emptied the till of cash and locked the money away in a safe built into a chimney-stack in his dining room. He had just removed the key from the safe door when he felt the gentle hand of his daughter touching his shoulder.

'The doctor says I'll be fit enough to ride again in a week or two,' she murmured, 'so please will you buy me another horse?'

Butch was never an easy touch at the best of times, and Daphne had chosen a bad moment to ask her father for such a favour.

'Dear girl! I've barely got enough money to buy dead animals to put on shelves in the shop without thinking of buying a live one for you to sit on and gallop round the fields. If things get any worse you'll have to go out to work and earn yourself a living.'

Daphne's tears were as much a result of the threat to her future as of her failure to secure another stallion. She was hurrying out of the house to conceal her distress when she encountered Bernard on his way to see her father and fled before he could speak to her.

'That daughter of yours was in a hurry,' said Bernard when Butch led him into the house. 'She looked as though she'd seen a ghost!'

'Guess what?' said Butch. 'She wants another horse!'

'Next time you'd better get her one that can jump fences.'

'Man! I can't afford to get her one at all. I told her she'll have to earn her own living soon and then she can buy what she likes.'

This explained to Bernard her reluctance to stop and speak to him. It was also comforting because he had come to ask her father to turn his field into a tourist attraction and he knew there would be opposition from Daphne if she were to go on keeping a horse there.

'It sounds like you'll be able to put that field to another use,' he said 'now that you'll not be keeping another horse in it.'

'There's not enough business to make it worth extending the car park, if that's what you mean.'

'No, George, I had a better idea. You could turn it into a tourist attraction. If you build a structure round the pit where the skeleton was found people will come and look at it, like they do Stonehenge, or Hadrians Wall.'

'My heart, boy, you've got some imagination! Who do you think will want to stare at an empty hole in the ground?'

'George, there are people who live in towns and cities who will come miles to be in the country for its fresh air and open skies. When they come to your field they'll get a bit of culture thrown in.'

'Aye, and I'll get a few other things thrown in if that's all they see!'

'Then we must make sure we give them something worth looking at.'

While Butch and Bernard were debating what to do about the field, Dr Chalmers was making plans to exhibit the bones at his university. When news of this leaked out (through some careless talk at the *Perch and Parrot)* there was indignation and uproar in the village. People who had no idea of the nature or value of what had been discovered insisted it ought to remain where it had lain for however long it had been there. A deputation went to see the parish chairman and demanded that he make a formal protest to the university.

Archie Thurrock was shy of dealing with a board of academics and decided instead to discuss it at a lower level with Evelyn.

'I suggest you let me bring Dr Chalmers to *The Willows,* said Evelyn when he spoke to her. 'We can then talk it over together in a peaceful atmosphere.'

Patrick Chalmers was reluctant, at first, to accept the invitation, for he inwardly resented Evelyn's blossoming relationship with the village dignitary. Evelyn persuaded him to change his mind by suggesting Mr Thurrock might have influence at the university. It was a disingenuous ploy, but sounded plausible enough. She knew that once he saw the inside of the house he would be impressed, and hoped he would forget to ask about the owner's possible connection with the university.

Archie Thurrock was equally impressed by having two scientific experts on the premises and did his best to be hospitable. He took them first into the library and offered them a drink before getting down to business. Then, when his guests were comfortably seated in large leather-lined armchairs, he stood with his back to the fireplace and assumed the role of parish chairman.

'I'm afraid people in the village will be offended,' he told them, 'if the bones are not returned after you have examined them.'

'You mean, put back in the ground again?' Dr Chalmers shook his head.

There was a long pause while Archie Thurrock thought.

'We could put them in a glass case where everyone can see them.'

'Like the *Perch and Parrot,* I suppose?' said Dr Chalmers.

There was another pause; then Archie made a magnanimous gesture.

'I could find room for them here at *The Willows* and keep open house on public holidays.'

'I would prefer to see them in a display cabinet at the University.'

Archie sensed his disappointment and said he would, of course, arrange for the doctor's name to be inscribed on the showcase.

'It would have to be a very large case,' said the doctor, 'or even several cases, because we don't know yet how much more we'll find as we work across the field.'

'It's not only what's in that field,' said Evelyn, anxious to make her own contribution to the argument. 'There could be items at the bottom of your garden which might be even more interesting than those bones at *The Brambles*.'

Archie's eyes lit up.

'You mean you've actually found something down there?' he gasped.

'Well, so far, only a few pieces of pottery, but that does suggest we may find more if we keep on looking.'

Archie listened, bemused, while the two scientists vied with each other to excite his interest and persuade him to let them carry on their investigations. They told him as much as they knew about what had been found, and Dr Chalmers explained why he had kept his options open about the age and nature of the animal bones. He confessed he had hoped to find a dinosaur but as he began to piece the remains together, he said, he realised they came from a mammal and not a reptile.

'Some of the bones,' he said, 'have now been sent for carbon dating.

Archie was not familiar with the expression and thought his leg was being pulled.

'What does that mean,' he asked, 'getting them branded, or put together again?'

Dr Chalmers explained.

'It's a scientific way of determining how old they are.'

Archie waved his leg mockingly at the doctor and said he knew all too well how old *his* bones were.

Dr Chalmers smiled. 'Let's hope no-one will need to know that in a hundred years from now!'

'Is that how old you think the mammal was?'

'I don't know, but it's not the age at which it died that I'm interested in. It's how long it is since it died that I want to know.'

Archie turned to Evelyn and asked if her pieces of pottery were getting the same treatment.

'Probably not,' she said, 'but people at the museum where I sent them will compare them with other pieces that have been dated already.'

Archie thought that was begging the question, but let it pass. He was now ready not only to house a series of display cabinets but, if necessary, to open *The Willows* to the public as a natural history museum.

Chapter 16

Business in the *Perch and Parrot* increased after Freddie joined the staff there. This was partly due to the presence of his friends, the Banner Boys, but also to regular visits from the scientists who were unravelling the past under the butcher's field opposite *The Brambles*. Dr Chalmers now employed an assistant and six of his students to enlarge the pit where bones were first uncovered, and they assembled in the bar each evening to discuss progress, and tactics for the following day.

After listening to one of these sessions the Banner Boys began to criticise the methods used by the scientists in their search.

'I reckon my old man would shift more earth in an afternoon,' said Billy, 'than those fellers from the university dig out in a week.'

'Don't forget they're looking for what's buried down there before they chuck the soil out,' said Tommy.

'They ought to do that first with a metal detector,' said Mathew, who had been reading about such methods.

Freddie reported the discussion to Amy, knowing she would tell her father.

'The boys think the scientists are using out-of-date methods in their work,' she told Bernard. 'If they had more modern equipment they could speed things up.'

Her father was impressed.

'Why don't you pass that message on to your friend Miss Oldfield?' he suggested. 'Or, better still, it might make a good radio programme.'

Amy thought about it, and asked her producer if she could take her recorder to the *Perch and Parrot*. This sounded at first like an excuse for a pub crawl but, when Amy told him what the Banner Boys had been saying, the prospect of a lively argument whetted his imagination. Arrangements were made with the publican for microphones to be installed and Dr Chalmers was invited to lead a discussion about what he was doing, and what he hoped to achieve.

Meanwhile, business at the supermarket was also flourishing.

Mr Grimley had been congratulated by his head office for increasing the turnover month on month. This was the result of widespread company advertising and increasing public awareness of what it was like to shop there. Customers liked the way goods were displayed. They enjoyed the wide avenues where they could steer their trolleys and admire the abundance of choice, both in terms of product and producer. (The concept of own-labelling had yet to come.) The novelty of being able to select and handle the goods before presenting them for payment enticed many shoppers to spend longer in the store and purchase more than would have been their custom elsewhere. Once so beguiled there were few who failed to return. Small shopkeepers in the vicinity saw their takings slump and one by one they faced the prospect of early closure.

In outlying villages shoppers continued to buy in small quantities and were satisfied to accept a smaller range of products from which to choose. Conversely, traders only stocked what their customers asked for. Modern marketing methods had yet to penetrate to rural areas and were slow to reach Backwater. It became clear that the decline in local trade was inversely proportional to the distance from a supermarket.

This might not have been the case had the Grimleys gone on living in the village. After the incident at the supermarket when fish were supposedly poisoned, head office had demanded the removal of staff living in Backwater and Mr Grimley imagined the restriction would apply to him. He therefore moved to a suburb half way between Backwater and the city, which reduced his travelling time and removed a threatened embargo.

Mrs Grimley was happy to move with her husband but loathe to forego the convenience of shopping occasionally at the *General Stores*.

'Why on earth should you want to go there,' asked Grimley, 'when you know I can bring home anything you want for the kitchen?'

Mrs Grimley said she sometimes wanted to be independent of what was sold in the supermarket.

'Do you mean you can buy things in that village shop which I don't sell?'

'Sometimes,' she said, 'but in any case I like the people who go there. And the people who own it,' she added.

Mr Grimley recalled the occasion of his only visit to the village shop and remembered why he had resolved to boycott it.

'You know I'd much rather you didn't go there,' he said, 'but if you must go, I do hope you'll be very careful what you say when you're in the shop.'

His wife said she knew he suspected the Talbot's daughter of sabotaging the supermarket, but said she was not trying to do the same to them.

'They might well think so,' said Mr Grimley, 'and one day they may accuse you of doing just that!'

Mrs Grimley thought for a moment, and raised her eyebrows.

'I have heard it said they think the supermarket has taken business away from the village.'

Mr Grimley changed the subject and decided he must find a way of getting his wife to do her shopping in future where he earned his wages. (He had not yet absorbed the fact that he was now a member of the salaried staff.)

Next morning, when he drove to work, the thought was still uppermost in his mind that he had to lure Mrs Grimley away from the village shop. Ideas for doing this were floating through his mind when he stopped before the traffic lights at a busy road junction. An unfamiliar sign on a lamp post caught his attention as he waited for the lights to change. Pointing towards the city, it said: THIS WAY TO THE SUPERMARKET. He resolved to tell his wife about it when he got home and remind her it was his wish that she should follow the sign instead of driving into the village to do her shopping. (He found later that the sign had been put there at the behest of his company as part of a campaign to enlarge the catchment area.)

When news of this reached Bernard he was most annoyed.

A few weeks later a similar notice appeared on the same lamp post, pointing in the opposite direction, saying: THIS WAY TO THE SUPER GENERAL STORES.

Neither sign had been approved by the planning committee and it was some months before anyone on the council noticed them. Because no-one had objected to them while they were up, no effort was made to take them down. Like a number of other road-signs they were frequently unheeded. Neither Bernard nor Grimley could genuinely claim to have detected an increase in business attributable to them so, to that extent also, they resembled other road-signs in that they remained in place long after their message became redundant; in fact, well beyond their sell-by date.

The *Perch and Parrot* filled rapidly on the night when *Radio Rustic* was due to broadcast a discussion led by Dr Chalmers. The Banner Boys were there in force, including Freddie who was allowed to stay on the customer side of the bar while the programme was on air.

Dr Chalmers began by saying how pleased he was to have an opportunity to tell everyone what had been happening, and he apologised for keeping them in the dark for so long.

'Aye,' said a wag in the audience, 'almost as long as them bones have been in the dark!'

Dr Chalmers responded by saying they now had a good idea just how long they had been in the ground.

'I'll come to that later,' he said, 'but first I want to explain how important it was to gather more evidence before the site got over-run by sightseers. It was difficult at first,' he said, 'to know what kind of creature we were dealing with because we only had a few bones to look at, but now we have an almost complete skeleton, and can say with fair certainty what it was that was buried there.'

'*Was* it a dinosaur?' asked a man who had heard the original rumours but not the denials.

'I heard it was a mammoth', said another, also out-of-date.

'Well it weren't a mouse!' cried the humorist among them.

Dr Chalmers was amused and asked if they wanted to run a sweep on it.

'They've done that already,' said the publican, who was listening eagerly from behind the bar.

'Well, in that case I'll tell you. But I think you'll be very surprised. It was a horse.'

There was a moment's silence, and then a roar of laughter.

'Not Daphne's surely?' said Freddie.

'No,' said the doctor, 'the one that got there first was buried 250 years ago.'

'There's no-one alive today who's that old, so how do you know that?' protested one of the disbelievers.

Dr Chalmers explained the technique of carbon dating which, he said, had been applied to the bones he sent to his university.

'The laboratory has just told me,' he announced, 'the result of their analysis.'

Mathew was excited. This sounded like a scientific method that would be more useful than a metal detector.

'If there was a horse in that field all that long ago,' he said, 'might there have been people as well, do you think?'

'A good question,' said Dr Chalmers. 'In all probability, yes, but my colleague, Miss Oldfield, is an archaeologist and she's looking for signs of habitation that would confirm it for us.'

The Banner Boys were delighted. This was news they thought would put their village in the spotlight, and open it up to curiosity and tourism. Bernard, who had been listening to the radio at home, was of the same opinion and hugged his daughter affectionately when she got home. Cynthia, as ever, was doubtful but admitted it was strange to think that people as well as horses might be buried at the bottom of their garden. She had forgotten that where she now lived there was no garden.

The garden at *The Willows* was looking more like a building site than a horticultural enterprise. The day after the broadcast Evelyn was there as usual supervising her team of volunteers searching for signs of an ancient community. Her mind, however, was not entirely on that subject. She was thinking more about the present. Archie had invited her to dine with him that evening.

This was the man she had once been told was haughty and difficult to get on with, but apart from their first meeting, when she thought he had been rather brusque, she had found him friendly and courteous. But she still knew very little about him. He seemed always to be alone in the house, yet it looked too well appointed to be the home of a bachelor. That evening, she decided, she would choose her moment carefully, and ask him if he was married or had been divorced.

The moment came when Archie offered brandy after they finished dinner.

The question did not surprise him. His wife, he said, had died in childbirth when she was very young and since then he had lived alone.

'I devoted myself to business,' he told her, 'and made enough money to retire in comfort. But now I'm getting on a bit I sometimes find it miserable sitting here on my own. That's why I'm glad of your company this evening. I hope you don't mind. Do, please, make yourself at home.'

Evelyn felt a little ashamed at raising the subject, but responded by looking around the room and admiring the furniture.

Archie watched her nervously and pointed to the sideboard where he had set a silver platter containing the specimens she rescued from his compost heap.

'Do you think you'll ever find more pottery where those pieces came from?'

Evelyn said she had searched in all the holes dug by the gardener before she came on the scene and nothing remotely historical had been discovered.

'We even enlarged the holes until they almost merged,' she told him.

Her host looked startled. It reminded him of the idea he once had to create a moat. Evelyn mistook his expression for one of anxiety.

'We didn't destroy any shrubs,' she assured him.

Archie said he would have been quite prepared to lose a few plants if it meant finding something worth keeping...'like a tomb, perhaps, or even a tomahawk!'

Evelyn seized on the remark. She said it was possible the artefacts she found in the compost had been thrown there by the gravediggers when they were preparing to bury Daphne's horse. In which case, she sighed, they might have come from the bottom of the pit.

'Oh dear! That means you'll want to exhume the horse, I suppose?'

'I doubt if we would get permission to do that,' said Evelyn, 'but I would like to dig another pit close by. Unfortunately that would mean transplanting some of your lovely roses.'

Archie said roses ought to prosper on the compost heap, and assured her she could go on digging as long as she liked.

Evelyn gave him a beautiful smile, and in response he offered to pay for the gravediggers to come back and repeat their excavation.

Sadly, Archie miscalculated the willingness of the vicar to discharge his gravediggers for such a task. The Reverend Lovelock was wholly unsympathetic.

'Those men,' he said, 'provide their labour to the church in the interest of putting the dead to rest and I simply cannot allow them to be used as scavengers!'

So, during the next few days, Evelyn and the gardener set to work with spades and barrows, digging deeper into the soil than either had ever dug before. At first they found nothing but stones and rubble, but as they cut a new trench between rows of Josephine Bruce and Ena Harkness they saw pieces of pottery which Evelyn thought might be remnants of an ancient urn that had once held oil or wine. If so, she could be sure an earlier folk had indeed inhabited the land on which they stood.

Chapter 17

Mathew tried in vain to purchase a carbon-dating machine. Hardware merchants advised him to look in the Yellow Pages and he telephoned a number of manufacturers who either thought he was playing a joke or directed him to a lonely hearts agency. In the end he gave up and settled for a hand held metal detector which he bought by mail order from a firm in Birmingham.

When Bernard heard this he said he was surprised the lad could afford it.

'When I was his age,' he said, 'it would have taken six months of my salary to buy something like that. Youngsters today get more in their wage packets than they know what to spend it on!'

Cynthia reminded him that times had changed in more respects than that.

'Everyone gets more money today than when we started out. Well, everyone, that is, who has a job. That's why we take more money here across the counter than shopkeepers did when we got married.'

'Aye,' said Bernard, 'but the real difference is that young people can *spend* more than we ever could. They don't have to part with most of it like we did to help our parents pay for food and rent.'

Cynthia said it was his fault that he didn't charge Amy for her keep while she lived at home, and Bernard said it wouldn't be fair so long as Jonathan was getting his keep for nothing. That led Cynthia to ask how much longer he thought it would be before Jonathan was qualified to earn a decent living.

'Give the lad a chance,' said his father. 'At least he's learning a trade.'

'I suppose that means you don't think Amy's got a future where she is.'

'I didn't say that, but she won't spend the rest of her life on the radio, will she?'

'How do you know that?'

'Well, she's a good-looking kid and she'll want to get married one day.'

Cynthia gave a deep-throated grunt, and complained she'd heard it all before: 'men work for a living and women work to look after them!'.

Luckily for Bernard there was a ring of the doorbell and they had a visitor.

George Trotter called to say there had been a development in the field where the bones had been discovered and the police had ordered him to close the car park.

'Whatever for? We haven't broken the law, have we? Don't tell me we needed planning permission!'

'No,' said George. 'Nothing like that. They've found more bones in the pit. Apparently they think these are human.'

The two men set off for the field where they found Dr Chalmers chatting with a police inspector. Nearby two constables were placing a tape across the entrance saying POLICE KEEP OUT.

Dr Chalmers apologised to Mr Trotter for inconveniencing his customers but said the discovery of human remains meant they were now in the hands of the civil authorities until the cause of death had been established.

'Do we know whose body it is?' asked Bernard.

'No,' said the inspector. 'Nor do we know how long it has been there.'

Dr Chalmers smiled. 'I think we do, inspector,' he said. 'About 250 years, I would say, give or take a year or two.'

The inspector looked suspicious, and said that would have to wait for the coroner.

When news reached *The Willows*, Evelyn was digging in the rose-beds aided by volunteers from the village who had offered their services free in the hope of seeing inside the parish chairman's residence.

'If you find any bones where you're digging,' Archie called to her, 'for goodness sake tell me first or we'll have policemen walking all over the estate.'

Evelyn confessed that the most interesting thing they had dug up recently was an old pipe which the gardener said may have been his.

Mention of a pipe reminded Archie that somewhere in the direction they were digging was a drain running from the house to a cesspit. When he told Evelyn of this the colour drained from her face.

'Oh dear,' she said, 'I thought there was a nasty smell when we started work this morning.'

So, it was not the police who called that afternoon, but the sanitary inspector from the district council.

Unaware of what was happening in the butcher's field or in Archie's garden, Mathew was busy learning how to operate his newly acquired piece of investigative equipment. After carefully reading the instructions he decided to make a practical test. First he borrowed a frying pan from the kitchen and then asked his friend Gerald to bury it on a plot of land near where he lived.

Fortunately the pan was not needed, nor its absence discovered, before it was detected and returned by Mathew to his mother's kitchen.

The test completed, Mathew called his friends together and set off with them to explore parts of the village not yet covered by the scientists.

'What are we looking for?' asked Lenny. 'That instrument is a metal detector. It won't recognise bones!'

'I know that,' said Mathew, 'but even if it did they wouldn't be worth anything to us. What we want to find is coins, and old bracelets, or pieces of gold, like they found in the tomb of Tutankhamen.'

Disparagingly, Tommy said he thought that was in Egypt. 'We're not going that far, are we?'

'There were burial chambers in England,' Mathew assured them. 'Only, I admit, they may not have mummies in them.'

Before any of them could wisecrack about where they might find mummies, there was a buzz on the metal detector.

'*Now* what do we do?' asked Gerald.

'Dig,' said Lenny.

Billy and Tommy were used to digging potatoes for their fathers on their allotments and they had brought spades and sacks in anticipation. So they set to work while their friends stood by and watched; which was what they had done when *their* fathers were digging for potatoes. Some minutes later, to everyone's delight, Billy unearthed a solid object covered in clay. Excitedly, they took it in turns to scrape the metal clean. Much to their disgust they could see it was a piece of farm machinery and threw it back, as fishermen do with a catch too small to eat.

Back home with his wife, Madeline, George Trotter was brooding over the latest catastrophe affecting their business. It was bad enough, he said, when they were having to deal with smears suggesting bones buried in the field opposite were ones he had thrown out from the butcher's shop, but now that human remains were being uncovered he dared not think what rumours would soon be circulating.

Madeline was convinced they would have to close the shop as well as the field and thought it might be opportune to go away for the holiday they had often promised themselves but never taken.

'That would only give credence to the rumours,' said Butch. 'People would think we were running away.'

'How can you say that?' asked his wife, 'It's not as if we'd murdered anybody.'

'Ah,' said Butch, 'but if somebody else has, people will want to know why they chose our field to dispose of the body.'

Domestic relations were already strained and neither husband nor wife wanted to pursue the argument. Also on their mind, and even more distressing, was what they thought was happening to Daphne. Instead of being prepared to take over the housekeeping so that her mother could help in the shop, or help in the shop herself, Daphne had taken a job at the garage working for Bobby Burns while his wife, Linda, was at home having another baby. Neither parent believed their daughter's motive was to lessen the burden of maternity for the Burns. They saw it as a means of being closer to the Talbot's son, Jonathan, who was now working at the garage daily and studying part-time at the technical college.

Madeline had the romantic idea that Daphne would be susceptible to thoughts of motherhood and therefore in danger of being seduced by Jonathan.

'If he's anything like you were at his age, she's bound to be in his sights by now!'

'Yes, but if she's anything like you are now, she'll know how to say no.'

It was a risky strategy, but when Butch caught sight of a glint in his wife's eyes he suggested they let the matter rest and take an early night to bed, to think it over.

There were no clouds on the horizon when Daphne and Jonathan finished work that evening. They were in a happy mood as they set off together down a narrow path between the harvest fields to a cottage where a notice on the gate said 'FRYING TONIGHT'. There they joined a small queue and bought portions of fish and chips from Chippy's wife who wrapped them in a copy of the previous day's newspaper. Too hot to eat immediately, they carried the meal to a nearby oak tree where they sat down on a patch of dry grass and feasted.

Daphne thought this might be a good moment to teach Jonathan what she believed he would never learn from a computer. So she offered him three wishes. He was still too inexperienced to recognise the ruse, and smiled naively as he answered.

'I wish I was five years older.'

'Why?' asked Daphne.

'Because then I would have finished studying and be free to do what I like each day.'

Daphne was about to comment when Jonathan said it was her turn now.

'You've two more wishes yet,' she said.

'We agreed to share everything, remember,' he told her. 'So now I want to hear your first wish.'

'I wish I could change my name,' she said, looking mischievously at him for a response.

116

'Don't you like Daphne?' he asked.

'No, and I don't like Trotter either.'

Jonathan failed to take the bait.

'Now it's my turn again,' he said. 'I wish I could fly.'

'Like a bird, or by aeroplane?'

'Like a buzzard, or an eagle.'

'How about a stork?'

Jonathan said it was Daphne's turn again.'

'OK. I wish I had another horse.'

'Have you asked your Dad for a replacement?'

'Ugh! That sounds like he ought to have kept spares. You've one wish left.'

'I wish I had a memory as good as my computer.'

'How do you know you haven't?'

Daphne placed her hand on his knee and squeezed it.

'Now can I have my last wish?' she cooed.

Jonathan raised his eyebrows and nodded.

'I wish we could stay here like this all night,' she murmured.

He looked down at her fingers, and a shiver trickled down his back.

'Wouldn't it be rather cold?'

'We could keep each other warm,' she said.

Which, although she did not know it, was what her mother and father were planning to do that night.

Chapter 18

When Amy passed the news to her programme editor that a human skeleton had been found in the butcher's field he recognised at once that this was no longer of local interest only but likely to attract media attention nationally. He knew Amy had handled the story well so far but decided this called for a more experienced reporter and said he would go there himself.

'Come on,' he said, 'show me the way and we'll go down to the field together before the big boys get there.'

Henry Christopher Coyle, known to his staff as C-C, got the impression from Amy's original broadcast that she and the archaeologist had jumped into a pit the size of a garden pond. When he and Amy entered the field it looked deserted and it was not until they reached the cordon which police had placed around the excavated area that he realised it was as large and deep as a municipal swimming pool. From the edge of the depression only the heads of people working below could be seen.

'Good heavens!' said C-C. 'Did you really jump in when you made that broadcast, or are there some steps?'

Amy led her editor to the shallow end and they descended to floor level without having to jump. There they were met by Dr Chalmers who was reluctant to show them around because he said the police were waiting to establish the cause of death of the person whose remains had been discovered.

The police had erected a tent over what remained.

Amy asked if they could see the body.

'There is no body to see,' said Dr Chalmers. 'All that's left under that tent is a bare skeleton.'

'Are they treating it as murder?' asked C-C, instinctively.

'Too soon to say,' said Dr Chalmers. 'A pathologist was here this morning to examine the skeleton. He confirmed that the bones were those of an old or middle-aged man, and said there were signs of injury, but he was not more specific.'

'Did he say how the man died, or even when?' asked C-C.

'No,' said Dr Chalmers, 'but I've got some views of my own about that.'

'Which I hope you are going to tell us,' said his interviewer.

'Well,' began the doctor, warming to the task. 'When we uncovered the skeleton of a horse, we noticed its hind legs were broken and the corpse had been covered with leaves and bracken. That suggested it may have fallen among trees in an overgrown wood, or else been buried there by somebody. Then, while we were looking to see if there were any other remains nearby, we stumbled on the bones under that tent which we recognised were human. For a time we wondered if we had unearthed an old cemetery, but as you can see, we have dug a long way out from where the man was buried and nothing else has come to light. My theory is that when the horse fell it threw its rider against a tree and both were killed. That would explain why their skeletons are some distance apart. In those days the wood was probably deserted and the bodies were never found – until your friend tried to bury her horse where one was buried already.'

'What a wonderful story,' said C-C. 'Can we broadcast that this evening before anyone else gets to hear it?'

'I doubt if I could stop you,' said Dr Chalmers. 'So do as you please!'

C-C put his hand on Amy's shoulder and smiled.

'Splendid,' he said. 'Now we'd better go back and read over the tape.'

Amy looked very uncomfortable.

'There's just one problem,' she said. 'I forgot to switch on the recorder.'

Dr Chalmers wanted to laugh, but pretended to be shocked. Mr Christopher Coyle was furious, but pretended to think it was funny.

'Never mind,' he said, 'Perhaps you'd be willing to come to the studio and we'll put you out live on our nightly news bulletin.'

This sounded more exciting than a canned version, and Dr Chalmers was easily persuaded.

The Banner Boys knew nothing about the impending broadcast which went out from *Radio Rustic* as they set out on their second sortie with the metal detector.

Mathew was confident that somewhere beneath the village they would find coins or bric-a-brac valuable enough to sell. His friends were unconvinced but enjoyed the fun of poking around with an unfamiliar instrument waiting for it to emit an unsociable sound.

They toured the lanes leading to the field opposite *The Brambles* and began walking towards *The Willows*, hoping they might strike a vein between the two places where relics had already been found. An hour passed without a bleep from the metal detector and signs of frustration set in. First Gerald and then Billy said they were dying for something to eat and it was agreed they should make for Chippy's. It meant trudging down a narrow steep-banked loke, past fields which had recently been harvested, to an open meadow where cattle grazed and clover grew. In the meadow they headed for the protruding roots of an ancient oak, known to them as a popular resting place. Tired now as well as hungry, the thought of sitting there to eat had sustained them on the way, but when they smelled the waft of frying fat coming towards them they realised someone had beaten them to it. Two other people were there already, dipping their fingers into a fist full of fish and chips.

Daphne and Jonathan were not expecting company but when they heard familiar voices they knew they would not be alone much longer.

'Can we join you?' asked Lenny, recognising old friends from schooldays.

'Sure,' said Daphne. 'But we haven't any chips to spare.'

'There wouldn't be enough to go round if you had,' said Billy. 'We're famished!'

'You'd better hurry up, then,' teased Daphne, 'before Old Chippy's fat gets cold.'

So the Banner Boys pressed on, and returned with their fish and chips, expecting to find the oak tree deserted.

'We're still here,' said Daphne. 'I want to make sure you don't leave your litter around, because we come here often and like to find it tidy.'

Billy caught sight of her grin, and retorted: 'Don't worry. We're so hungry we'll eat everything, including the paper.'

Jonathan was a little embarrassed by the banter and drew attention to Mathew swinging what looked like an unfurled umbrella.

'Is that a metal detector?' he asked.

Mathew said it was a magnetometer.

'Does it work?' asked Jonathan.

By way of an answer Mathew pressed the on switch, and to everyone's surprise the instrument began to buzz.

Billy and Lenny hurriedly finished their fish and chips, grabbed the golfer's buggy which they had been dragging round with them, took from it a pickaxe and shovel, and set about digging. Gerald and Tommy followed shortly afterwards with the spade and fork that were also in the buggy. Noise from the metal detector rose and fell in intensity as Mathew marched up and down around the oak tree. Daphne and Jonathan shouted encouragement while digging continued in all directions. Suddenly, with a cry of *eureka*, Lenny pulled from the soil a mud-splattered bracelet.

'Looks like you dropped something,' he said, handing it to Daphne. 'Did you take off anything else we might find?'

Daphne rushed across to slap his face, but thought better of it and grabbed the bracelet.

'Never seen it before,' she said. 'But as you won't be wearing it, I'll look after it.'

Meanwhile Billy went on enlarging the hole where Lenny found the bracelet and a few minutes later he produced from the mud a dull and dirty coin.

'This might be yours,' he called to Jonathan. 'Must have slipped out of your trouser pocket,' he grinned.

Jonathan blushed and stared hard at the coin.

'I've never seen one like that before,' he said. 'I'd say it was very old, or maybe foreign. Look, see for yourself, there's no queen's head on it!'

Mathew was excited. 'I guess we've struck treasure,' he cried.

Later that evening, as the sun went down, Daphne and Jonathan went to their respective homes, but the five Banner Boys made for the *Perch and Parrot* where they told their story to Freddie.

The bar was not busy and they were overheard by one of the customers.

'If you need any help tomorrow,' said Evelyn Oldfield, moving closer to make herself known, 'I'm an archaeologist and I'm willing to bring my students and advise you on what you've found.'

Lenny was on the verge of dismissing the eavesdropper when Freddie recognised who she was.

'I thought you were working at *The Willows*,' he told her. 'I heard a rumour you've not found much there lately.'

Evelyn said it was true, but that she hadn't given up hope of finding more.

'It sounds,' she said, 'as if you've been a bit luckier.'

'If we did find something valuable, would there be a reward?' asked Mathew.

'That depends,' said Evelyn. 'If no-one else claims it belongs to them, you may be able to keep what you find. On the other hand, if there is a lot of it, it becomes Treasure Trove and the coroner has to decide if it belongs to the Crown. In that case you would have to hand it over. You might then get a reward for finding it, or you might be allowed to keep it.'

Lenny saw the drift of Mathew's question.

'If you and your students were to help us,' he asked, 'would we have to share the reward?'

Evelyn smiled and said that might depend on who did most of the digging.

'We got here first,' said Mathew, 'so, technically, anything that's found down there ought to be ours.'

Evelyn made no attempt to dispute the fact but reminded the boys their next job ought to be to find out who owned the land and report their findings to the landlord.

They said they thought the clearing where they made their discovery belonged to the parish.

Evelyn said she would speak to the parish chairman about it.

'It is quite possible,' she added, 'that between us we may find more buried articles and reveal an old settlement where your ancestors used to live. In which case we'll want to extend the dig into the fields nearby. Do you know who those fields belong to?'

'Yes,' said Gerald. 'It's old Prickly Berry. He 'on't want to part wi' anything wot's worth a bob or two!'

Freddie said he knew someone who might be able to help them in that respect.

'You all know who I mean,' he said. 'Mr Talbot has dealt with Prickly before, and I'll ask him if he will do so again.'

Freddie was not expecting to see Amy that evening because she had told him she would be working late at the studio. It was a surprise, therefore, when she walked in to the *Perch and Parrot* just as he was contemplating how to ask her father to persuade Farmer Berry to let them into his field.

'Talk of the devil! Here comes his daughter!' he shouted, but before he could tell her what they had been talking about Amy shook her head.

'I need something quick to cheer me up,' she pleaded. 'I've done something terrible and I'm in disgrace with my bosses.'

A drink was quickly dispensed while she told them what had happened, or rather not happened, with the tape recorder. They were sympathetic, but anxious to tell her what the boys had discovered under the oak tree near the fish and chip shop. At first she showed more interest in the news that her brother was there with Daphne, but when she heard of the items they found under the ground her mood changed. She could tell C-C in the morning, and he would see they had another scoop on their hands. Surely, she thought, he would forgive her now for the sin of not switching on the recorder.

Next morning Freddie met Evelyn at *The Willows* to show her the way to the oak tree. Before he arrived to collect her she spoke to the chairman and got his approval to dig on ground belonging to the parish.

'He made me promise,' she told Freddie; 'not to obstruct a public right of way along the footpath, and to replace the soil we remove during excavation.'

When they reached the site Evelyn was surprised to see how much soil had already been removed. She was also horrified to find the boys had left open the holes they dug the night before. Some of the holes were deep enough to trap in the dark any unsuspecting passer-by.

'You must scold your friends,' she said, 'for failing to protect the public.'

'I don't suppose many people come this way in the dark,' said Freddie. 'There's an old superstition about a tree that's haunted and folk say ghosts have been seen there at night.'

Evelyn was about to dismiss the idea of superstition when her attention was drawn to a real-life figure seen coming towards them across an adjacent field.

'Look out!' said Freddie. 'Here comes the farmer we told you about.'

'Mr 'Prickly' - what did you say his name was?'

'Berry,' said Freddie.

Evelyn called to him across the hedge. 'Good morning, Mr Berry.'

The farmer responded by staring first at the visitors and then at the holes.

'Did I hear you say you were going to bury somebody?' he asked.

'Sorry!' said Evelyn. '*We* didn't dig those holes, by the way.'

'Then it were a pretty big badger!'

'But we do know who did dig them,' said Evelyn.

She then told him what the boys had discovered.

'You mean there's treasure down there in them holes?'

'Yes,' said Evelyn, 'and maybe there'll be more under your field if you'll permit us to look.'

Mr Berry shed his prickles. What neither Freddie nor Evelyn knew was that 'Prickly' had just enjoyed a successful season, with bumper crops of strawberries, raspberries, blackcurrants, and gooseberries, and was about to spend his profits on a Caribbean Cruise. News that the land which had produced such fruit might yet yield more, if treasure lay beneath it, was enough to ensure agreement to Evelyn's request.

'I've gathered this year's harvest,' he said, 'so you can dig where you like – so long as you put back the soil afore it's time to sow next year's crop.'

Chapter 19

Evelyn's success in dealing with a difficult farmer was quickly forgotten when she studied the site to which Freddie had brought her. She soon saw it was not a matter of following on where the Banner Boys had left off because there were no marks to show where they found the items they had lifted. Her first task, therefore, was to establish a frame of reference. This meant getting her students to create an enclosure in the shape of a rectangle. Posts were erected and aligned on a compass bearing, and their location marked on a large scale Ordnance Survey map of the area. Anything they unearthed thereafter could be measured from the corner posts and recorded with a grid reference.

When that was done they were ready to resume excavating.

By the time the boys got back to the site in the evening they had each completed a day's work, for which they earned money, whereas Evelyn's volunteers had dug and scraped all day around the oak tree for the pleasure of it. What had been a collection of humps and hollows at the edge of a wood the previous night now looked more like the foundations for a large house or factory. The boys stood in wonder and struggled to remember how it was when they last saw it.

'Looks like someone's been busy!' said Billy, recovering his breath.

Lenny nudged Billy's arm.

'You don't suppose she's dug all that up to look for worms, do you?'

Evelyn overheard the remark and smiled.

'Yes, you could say I've been fishing, I suppose. But what I've been looking for is anything that will show if there were people or animals here a very long time ago. That's why we have to look carefully at every level below the surface, and not just dig a series of holes like you were doing.'

'We only dug a hole where the metal detector told us to,' said Mathew.

'I know,' said Evelyn, 'but there may be plenty of other interesting things down there that aren't made of metal.'

'Like what?' asked Gerald.

'Bones,' said Evelyn, 'or pottery; even old bricks and stonework where people used to live. Anything that got overgrown and buried after years of neglect.'

The boys stared at each other and looked bemused.

'Is there anything left for us to do?' asked Gerald, hoping perhaps that he could go home now.

Evelyn told them they had only just begun.

'Since you left,' she said, 'you'll be pleased to know we have uncovered some more objects. You'll find them all labelled and dated in a box over there by the side of the tree, waiting to go to the university tomorrow for examination.'

Lenny said he thought they were looking for something to sell.

'Maybe,' said Evelyn, who knew that this was the prime objective of most amateur archaeologists, 'but everything has to be identified and valued first.'

Mathew looked indignant.

'It seems I'd have done better to buy a pencil sharpener!' he moaned.

Evelyn now realised she had taken for granted the boys' enthusiasm and underestimated their expectation of reward.

'I think,' she said, 'we may be looking for different things. But don't worry – they're not incompatible. I'm sure the magnetometer cost a lot of money, and I know it will still be useful. However, I can't promise it will pay for itself all at once.'

'You haven't told us yet what objects you put in that box,' said Lenny. 'Were they interesting?'

'Yes, they were,' said Evelyn. 'We uncovered a small leather bag which might have been a purse; possibly the one from which your coin was dropped. Then we came upon a brooch and a silver necklace, which could have belonged to the lady who lost a bracelet.'

'Somebody must have dropped them,' said Lenny, thoughtfully. 'In that case, we'd better keep on digging, 'cos there might be another body.'

Evelyn said she very much hoped they would all go on digging.

'When you see signs of something buried in the soil I'll show you how to extract it with a trowel and a toothbrush.'

The boys laughed, but as they had not brought toothbrushes they flourished the picks and shovels which they did have with them. Evelyn was anxious to have their support but wary of the damage they might do with such equipment.

'I tell you what,' she said 'why don't you walk over the ground we've been digging today and if your detector gives out any signals we'll dig there.'

Mathew had lost much of his eagerness to lead and he fell behind the others as they trudged across the site. In spite of some boisterous shouts and bawdy singing by those ahead of him, he and the magnetometer remained silent. The sun sank slowly over the horizon, and morale went with it. Together they put a cordon round the site, lit the paraffin burners, and made their separate ways home for the night.

In bed that evening, Evelyn took stock of her position. Working with Dr Chalmers in a field near *The Brambles* she had seen nothing but bones; in Archie's garden at *The Willows* there were shards of pottery, but a strong suspicion they had been imported from elsewhere. A museum had confirmed her belief that the pottery was Early Saxon, but the bones had been proved by carbon-dating to belong to the eighteenth century. What they were now finding near the oak tree was more of an age with the bones than the pottery and she realised her dream of finding a Saxon enclave in the village was fading fast.

Next morning, in the butcher's field, Dr Chalmers and the coroner were conferring over the excavated bones of a man and a horse. The coroner accepted evidence that the injuries to beast and man had probably resulted from accidental falls that occurred perhaps more than a couple of hundred years ago, and gave his permission for the skeletons to be removed. Photographs were taken, and arrangements made for the bones to be lifted and displayed at the university, pending a decision about their final destination.

Meanwhile, at *The Willows*, where the parish chairman still hoped to house the remains of everything found buried below the village, Archie was worrying about the absence of his lady archaeologist.

'Has she quit digging?' he asked the gardener, 'or is she just taking time off to be with those young lads and their metal detector?'

The gardener said he thought she was losing faith about finding any more relics at *The Willows*.

'Something I said to her made her think the bits of pottery we found here may have come with a load of topsoil I brought in a couple of seasons ago.'

Archie looked upset, but curious.

'Where did you put it?'

'Among the roses.'

'Do you know where the topsoil came from?'

'No,' said the gardener, 'but it weren't much good for the roses!'

Archie went back into the house and revised his ideas about converting part of it into a museum. Later that week he drove to the county council offices and sought consolation from the resident historian.

Mr Balderwood, the historian, greeted Archie as an old friend and they spent the afternoon browsing through old records and maps of the neighbourhood, searching for clues that might tell them what life had been like in Backwater before any of its present inhabitants were born.

They had almost given up hope of finding any reference to an ancient settlement in the vicinity, when the historian found a passage in an ancient diary which mentioned a wood through which coachmen were prone to take short-cuts when travelling between the neighbouring cities. The track, it said, was popular because it enabled coachmen to make up time lost when they stayed too long at a wayside inn. According to the diarist, it was frequented by highwaymen, and many rich passengers were robbed *en route* to their destination. There was nothing in the story that identified it with Backwater but Archie thought it would appeal to Bernard. No doubt there were similar tracks in many parts of the county where highwaymen operated and there was no reason to suppose that Backwater had been an exception.

Archie had just got back from the County Library when the doorbell at *The Willows* rang. Thinking it might be Bernard delivering groceries he intended to tease him by suggesting he was about to experience another highway robbery. Instead, he opened the door to Evelyn.

'Hallo Archie. I expect you must think I've deserted you. Do forgive me.'

The parish chairman tried to look as though no such thought had ever entered his head.

'Come in, dear lady,' he said. 'I'm sure there's been a good reason.'

Leading her into his study he offered her a drink and poured one for himself.

'Thank you,' she said. 'I'll make that one for the road.''

Archie looked puzzled.

'Does that mean you're in a hurry to be off again?'

'No,' said Evelyn, 'it means I have something exciting to tell you.'

Archie now looked serious.

'Has it, perchance, anything to do with our friend Dr Chalmers?'

'In a way, yes – but only indirectly. You see, I think we've located an old road that used to run through the village. What's more,' she added, 'it looks as if it passed through the butcher's field where Dr Chalmers is working. So, if that proves to be the case, his theory about the man and the horse having fallen together, and then died there, could be right.'

Archie listened now with growing interest.

'Do you know,' he said, 'I think I can add to that theory. What would you say if I suggested the dead man might have been a highwayman?'

He then told her what he and the historian had been reading that afternoon. They both agreed it was a plausible explanation and raised their glasses to acknowledge the importance of the discovery.

However, they had yet to learn what had been discovered at *The Brambles*.

On her way home from the garage that evening Daphne saw a Landrover speeding across her father's field into the excavated area beyond the car park. Out of curiosity, she decided to follow it. When she reached the point where it stopped she was in time to see Dr Chalmers and his students packing a number of shallow boxes into the vehicle. Believing the boxes to contain the bones of both skeletons found on the site she rushed forward to resist. As she did so she stumbled on a ridge of mud churned up by the Landrover and caught sight of a gleam of light coming from under her feet near the back wheel of the car.

Bending down, she scraped at the soil with her fingers and unearthed a small metal object which she picked up and rubbed with the palm of her hand. As the mud fell away from the metal she saw to her horror that she was holding a grubby but well preserved pistol.

Dr Chalmers looked as if he had been shot by it when Daphne took it to him, for it now cast doubt on the coroner's verdict and opened up the possibility that they might, indeed, have uncovered the victim of a murder.

Chapter 20

Evelyn was keen to meet Dr Chalmers in the public house that evening because she wanted to tell him about her discovery of an ancient road. The news, however, was quickly trumped by Dr Chalmers when he told her about the pistol.

Once they recovered from the impact of these revelations the two scientists settled down to evaluate the implications. They agreed that the evidence appeared to support the theory of a horse having thrown its rider while galloping along a track where articles of jewellery and money had been dropped. The possibility of armed robbery by a highwayman had now to be considered.

Evelyn was ready to believe the dead man had been the highwayman who shed some of his loot while making off in a hurry, then had the misfortune to be thrown and dropped his pistol as he fell off the horse.

Chalmers demurred. He said the dead man could have been a victim of the highwayman.

'In that case,' said Evelyn, ' there would have been two men, but we've only found one body.'

'Maybe the highwayman got away!'

'On a dead horse?'

'The horse could have belonged to the dead man.'

'Who dropped the pistol...'

'Yes.'

'So you think there was another man, on another horse, and another pistol?'

'No; I just think there might have been.'

'Why don't we stick to the evidence we've collected?'

'OK, but there's more than one way to interpret it.'

'Sure! But there's no evidence that a shot was fired.'

'Or of there being a highwayman.'

'Well, how do you explain the trail of treasure strewn along the track?'

'It could have been dropped there accidentally.'

'So, the dead man, dead horse, and pistol are unconnected? Just coincidental!'

'We'll never know,' said Dr Chalmers. 'I doubt if there are fingerprints on the jewellery, or the weapon, and there won't be any on the skeleton, so we shan't know who they belonged to.'

Evelyn was tired. 'Alright,' she said, 'I can't see that it matters. There won't be any relatives alive to claim the treasure.'

'Or witnesses to prove what happened.'

Dr Chalmers had the last word. He then emptied his glass and placed his hand on Evelyn's shoulder. 'A more immediate question,' he said, 'is whether the coroner will want to reopen the case when he gets to know about the pistol?'

While the debate, or dispute, was going on in the *Perch and Parrot* Daphne called at the *General Stores* and Bernard overheard her talking to Amy.

'There was a truck in the field and I went over to see what it was doing there. As I got closer I saw it was being loaded with little boxes. Then I noticed something sticking out of the mud under a back wheel. I thought it must have dropped from one of the boxes and was about to hand it to them when I realised what it was.'

At this stage Bernard was more interested in what was in the boxes than what might have dropped from them. He guessed they were probably full of the bones which he wanted to remain in the village, and he was angry because he considered they were being stolen. When he heard Daphne mention a pistol and say Dr Chalmers thought there might have been a murder, his mood changed and he was delighted.

'Come and listen to the good news,' he called to Cynthia. 'There may have been a murder in the village hundreds of years ago. We might have a place in the history books yet.'

Cynthia was not impressed.

'I doubt if anyone will care, unless it happened yesterday; and then only if it was particularly gruesome!'

Bernard said he thought it would make a jolly good story.

Amy did not need her father's enthusiasm to tell her she had another scoop on her hands. She and Daphne were already on their way to the radio station.

Excited, and out of breath, they were just in time to catch the last news bulletin of the evening.

Neither Amy nor Daphne had been in the *Perch and Parrot* when Evelyn was telling Dr Chalmers what she had learned from Archie Thurrock, so there was no reference in the broadcast to any hint of a highwayman. All that was mentioned over the air was the discovery of a pistol and the possibility that the dead man and a horse had been the victims of a murder.

By next morning, the village was awash with rumour. Many inhabitants heard the story second-hand, and some only heard a part of the broadcast. The fact that it related to an event many generations ago did not deter them from repeating it. When Archie and the two scientists heard what had been reported they got *Radio Rustic* to tell the full story in their next bulletin the following day. For the first time the villagers of Backwater heard about the legend of highway robberies on a road which had since been buried under their feet.

Within hours of hearing that the dead man may have been a highwayman, reporters from national newspapers and television companies descended on the village, demanding interviews with Dr Chalmers and any local character prepared to give them a story. The headline in one newspaper the following morning had a distinctly Agatha Christie look about it. 'MURDER ON A HIDDEN HIGHWAY,' it said, with a diagram placing the village on a road to nowhere.

For a few days, strangers appeared in the village asking the way to the historical site, but the curiosity was short-lived and nobody stayed long enough to add much to the income of local traders.

Contrary to Bernard's expectation, it was not the possibility of a murder in the neighbourhood which attracted most attention but the prospect of finding valuables hidden in the soil. All over Backwater spades were in action as men of all ages dug holes in their gardens and trenches in allotments, not to plant flowers or vegetables, but in the hope of finding artefacts to sell. The market, it was said, was museums, Americans and antique dealers. Bernard could remember his father quoting the wartime slogan 'Dig for Victory'; but a new craze in the village was digging for treasure.

The Banner Boys continued their sorties with Mathew and his metal detector but soon tired of exploring the old road which Evelyn had uncovered. They readily accepted an invitation from Dr Chalmers to search around the area where Daphne had found the pistol in case his team of helpers had overlooked anything of interest or value which might support his hypothesis of a second gunman. Apart from a few false alarms, they failed to corroborate the doctor's theory.

While they were scanning over the site the coroner came to see where the pistol had been found and, much to Dr Chalmers' relief, he saw no reason to hold an inquest. He did, however, ask what the boys were doing and chatted with them about their equipment. Flattered by the coroner's interest, Mathew took the opportunity to ask his permission to keep the items they had found elsewhere.

'You'll have to come to my office and fill out a form before I can grant you that,' he told them. 'In the meantime you ought to bring me everything you've recovered so far.'

'That'll teach you to keep your mouth shut!' said Gerald.

Meanwhile, Evelyn was at *The Willows* asking Archie, as chairman of the parish council, for permission to preserve the stretch of road she had helped to excavate.

'You must know,' he told her, 'it is not in my power to do that. But in any case, it's not exactly the kind of thing you can put on display in a museum, or cover over with a pane of glass. So, how were you thinking of preserving it?'

'I thought if we completed the excavation it might be put back into use.'

'Have you any idea how long it was, or where it went to?'

'No,' said Evelyn, 'but we would find out if we kept on digging.'

Archie was not enthusiastic. He remembered how she had given up on the holes in his garden and left his gardener with a lot of filling in to do.

'I'll think about it,' he said.

'If you've got an Ordnance Survey map of the area,' said Evelyn, not yet ready to give up, 'we can probably work out where the road came from and where it was going.'

Archie frowned, but reluctantly fetched the map and laid it out on the library table. Evelyn thanked him sweetly and asked if she could mark on it the section of road that was now exposed. Melting slowly as her perfume reached him, Archie handed her a yellow highlighter and watched her trace a straight line between the field in front of *The Brambles* and a field owned by Farmer Berry.

'That much we can be sure,' said Evelyn. 'And, if we project it beyond the butcher's, you can see it joins up with the old road to the coast...'

'And in the other direction?' Archie was ahead of her.

'Straight into the city,' she said. She beamed because she felt sure it would be an amenity for those now living in the village.

Archie did not share her enthusiasm.

'Do you see what part of the city it leads to?' he asked.

Evelyn guessed from his expression there was something she had overlooked.

'Dear lady,' he sighed, 'you'd better not tell the grocer where it would lead to, for that is where they built a supermarket.'

When Bernard heard what Evelyn had proposed, and where the road would lead to, he thought it was a joke.

'Now pull the other one!' he said.

He was assured it was true.

Bernard fell silent. Was a voice out there trying to tell him something? If so, he knew it already. 'Plus ça change!' as his father used to say. Where the old road used to go, a new road now ran to the city; where highwaymen once robbed travellers as they passed through the village, now it was the supermarket operators who were robbing the shopkeepers of Backwater.

He called on his friend George Trotter for sympathy, and to give him the news, but Butch had already heard. Evelyn had been to see him early that morning asking for his support to keep the old road open now that it had been uncovered.

'You didn't agree with her, I hope,' said Bernard. 'You know where that road goes to, I suppose?'

'Aye, she told me. I guess you think it's a bad omen.'

'Omen? No, it's a diabolical insult! Folk don't need another road to take them to the supermarket. Too many people are doing their shopping there already.'

Butch looked uncomfortable.

Bernard thought perhaps he'd been too abrupt.

'She's a very persuasive lady,' he said. 'And I expect she's very proud of what she's discovered.'

'There's something I ought to tell you,' said Butch, spluttering badly. 'I've been meaning to call and see you, but it's all happened rather suddenly. Business has been very poor recently, as you know. Well, I've decided to close the shop at the end of the month.'

Bernard had feared the day would come, but didn't expect it at that moment.

'What will you do? Sell up and move out of the village?'

Butch hesitated, and then confessed.

'I've accepted an offer to go and work for somebody else for a change.'

'That *would* be a change,' said Bernard. 'I can't see you wanting to cut meat with blokes who haven't yet cut their teeth. Besides, there's not another butcher in the village, so where did you find one brave enough to take you on?'

'There's a place in the city where they need someone to start up a new department. That's why the idea of a short-cut from the village appealed to me when I heard about it.'

'I suppose a short-cut to a butcher,' said Bernard, trying to make light of a dark subject, 'is like saying buzz off to a bee-keeper!'

George Trotter did not laugh. He waited until Bernard had taken the grin from his face and then dropped his bombshell.

'I shall be in charge of a fresh meat counter at the supermarket.'

Blood rushed to Bernard's cheeks. He saw a knife in front of him and would dearly have loved to thrust it into the butcher.

At the other end of the village, happier news was being conveyed to Bernard's son, Jonathan. Bobby Burns, his employer, had become a father. Linda Burns had given birth to a boy and told Daphne Trotter, her understudy at the garage, that she could carry on working there because she intended to stay at home and look after the baby.

Cynthia realised as soon as Bernard walked through the door that something had seriously upset him. Without saying a word, he helped himself to a drink and flopped into an armchair, his hands visibly trembling.

'Whatever is the matter? You've had some bad news, haven't you?.'

'George Trotter is a traitor!'

Cynthia waited for the explanation.

'He's closing his shop in the village and going to work at the supermarket.'

'Oh dear! Where shall we get our meat? I'm not going into Grimley's to get it!'

'And I'm not going to be a vegetarian! We'll have to start selling meat from here in future.'

'That's all very well, but where would we keep it?'

'We'll have to buy another freezer.'

'Where would we put it?'

Cynthia wanted to help her husband, for she knew he had been dreadfully hurt, but the more they fantasised about the remedy the less practical it seemed.

Then Bernard made a startling recovery.

'I know what we can do,' he said, leaping out of the armchair. 'We'll clear the shelves of all the slow-moving items, like they do in the supermarket, and make room for a new and massive deep freezer. That way we'll play the supermarket at their own game and make damn sure none of old Butch's customers from the village has to struggle into the city to get their Sunday joint.'

It was the beginning of a new era at Backwater and a new look for the *General Stores*. Life in the village would never be quite the same.

Chapter 21

For many people in Backwater life was now very different from when Harry and Mildred Talbot handed over the *General Stores* to their son and daughter-in-law. The village was no longer remote from what was happening elsewhere in the country, yet it still had a long way to go to catch up. Bernard and Cynthia had lived in the suburbs of a big city before they moved to the country and they brought to the village their experience of shopping in the metropolis, but more substantial changes reflected the influence on local taste and behaviour of current advertising in the media.

Young people adapted more readily to these changes, and it became a problem for the Talbots to maintain supplies of what their older customers wanted while adding newer products to satisfy the young. However, many of the younger generation had already left the village to seek adventure and employment in larger communities and the young families that remained were mostly related to older residents who had lived in the village all their lives.

There were no incentives for young people, with or without families, to move in from other parts of the country.

Imperceptibly, the pattern of life, as in all rural areas, was modified as modern equipment and technology became affordable to all. The welfare state supported people who might otherwise have been obliged to endure the less comfortable lifestyle familiar to their ancestors. Even the smallest of cottages now had electricity and television, tapwater and public drainage.

As old folk died their properties were often bought by city dwellers only slightly less old who were seeking a place for retirement. Demand of this kind far outstripped supply and prices rose to levels that only the well endowed could afford. This also meant that young people who had not already flown the nest but wanted to start families of their own were unable to buy houses in the village.

Bernard's campaign to resist the arrival of a supermarket was not an attempt to avert change, but an act of self-defence as a rural shopkeeper. It was clear from the beginning that his views were not shared by the whole community but his prophesy that competition on such a scale would eventually deprive the village of its own shops was about to come true.

Once George Trotter closed the butcher's shop it was not long before Doughie, the baker, and Charlie Plumstead, the milkman, followed suit. Doughie managed to persuade Mr Grimley to install bread-making ovens at the supermarket and, in Bernard's eyes, he became another 'deserter'. Charlie had nowhere else to go and simply retired, leaving the village without its daily delivery of milk. For a time this added business to the *General Stores*, but it also lead to more people shopping for all their goods outside the village.

It took Bernard a very long time to admit it, but he had to recognise there were many features of the supermarket that appealed to its customers and once people from the village sampled them they invariably returned for more.

The very sight of a superstore created an atmosphere of opulence. Inside, the customer was overwhelmed with choice and the freedom to roam. There were avenues of shelves filled with countless items of tantalising variety, and there was always a trolley with the inducement to load it with as many goods as it would hold. Not surprisingly, many people purchased more than they intended, or even needed.

A shopping expedition of this kind was usually a satisfying experience, and it often included an element of adventure in the discovery of new products, or the making of new friendships. For some people it became a habit and that was what every supermarket manager strove to achieve. In that respect Mr Grimley was successful because there were no competitors in the neighbourhood with comparable facilities to offer.

He did not, however, have an easy life.

Like Bernard he had to face the fact that for many people the way of life was changing. Not only were there vastly more goods that people could buy, and new ways by which they could pay for them, but the manner of selling had become aggressive and combatant.

When Mr Grimley first opened the supermarket if somebody had mentioned a bar code he would have thought they were talking about a new rule for publicans. Yet the barcode was soon to revolutionise the retail business. New equipment had to be installed, designed to eliminate human error at the cash points, and reduce the time and labour devoted to stock control. For Mr Grimley it meant working overnight and all weekend while new tills were introduced and staff trained to use them. For customers it meant a speedier passage through the check-outs but, as so often with technical innovations, it also meant the loss of a previous facility. The diligent were no longer able to check for themselves how much they were being charged for individual items.

To overcome customers' criticism of this a new model was produced which issued itemised receipts, and that resulted in the manager suffering another lost weekend to install it.

Then came credit cards and loyalty cards, and yet more changes of equipment for the manager to deal with. The credit card became popular when inflation reached double figures and the cost of goods outstripped the capacity of pockets and handbags to hold the amount of money needed for a shopping expedition. Banks were the first to benefit, because they charged the retailers for each transaction, and customers also if they were slow to repay the debt. Many retailers objected to sharing their profit margin with the bank, but supermarkets soon recognised that credit cards encouraged people to spend not only more than the amount of cash they were carrying but often more than they could really afford. To prevent this discouraging anybody from coming again, loyalty cards were offered to regular customers rewarding them with rebates on accumulated purchases.

There was, though, one type of change which Mr Grimley rather enjoyed, especially as it did not call for any new machinery. By moving goods which sold slowly into positions where customers had to pass them in order to reach the more popular items, people were tempted to buy things they had not intended to buy while searching for what they really came for.

For all its vicissitudes, management of the supermarket appealed to Mr Grimley. In spite of its pressures and stresses, his life was no less eventful than Bernard's, and he enjoyed the great advantage over his rival in that he had a regular salary and a large staff to share his burdens.

Once Amy and Freddie had been discharged by Mr Grimley, Bernard had no knowledge of his competitor's prices until some of his customers bought goods in the supermarket and told him how much more he was charging for them in the *General Stores*. Then, as their visits to the supermarket became more frequent, he realised from his customers' remarks, that he had more important things to attend to than price. People were getting accustomed to a different technique of shopping, and he knew if he wanted to survive he would have to rearrange his shelves and redesign the lay out so they could pick and choose at will. The problem was, how could he do this with the limited space at his disposal.

139

Sometimes the solution to a problem comes in a flash, sometimes in a dream, and often as a stroke of luck. In Bernard's case it could be said that it came, sadly and suddenly, as two strokes. Within a few weeks of each other, both his mother and then his father suffered coronaries and died, leaving vacant their house next door.

Cynthia allowed a respectable interval, and then suggested it would be better if she and Bernard were to move in to his parents' house and extend the shop over what had been their living room and kitchen on the ground floor. This was agreed and the shop was closed for two weeks while alterations were carried out. Shelving was built in parallel bays down the enlarged floor area so that customers could stroll and select their goods at leisure. A new window on to the street was fitted to provide more space for revealing what was available inside, and above the window a large illuminated sign was hung with the new name by which they wished to be known.

No longer the *General Stores*; they were now:

THE VILLAGE SUPERSTORES.

Amy reported the event for *Radio Rustic*, but went over the top in describing it. She had never been fully forgiven for the gaffe she made with a tape recorder and for the second time in her life she was sacked. It transpired that Mr Christopher Coyle was a shareholder in the company which owned the supermarket.

Bernard had never liked the idea of his daughter spending the rest of her life as a radio reporter and he greeted the news of her dismissal as an opportunity to lure her into the family business.

'You know the time will come,' he told her, 'when your mother and I will want to give up the shop and we've always hoped you or your brother would take it over like we did from my parents.'

Amy could see what was coming, but allowed her father to continue.

'I know you've helped out from time to time, but what do you say to joining us full time, as a member of staff? I can pay you a proper wage now we've enlarged the premises.'

'Could you afford to pay for two of us?' she asked.

Bernard supposed she thought he had made the same offer to Jonathan.

'Your brother has always said he is not interested.'

'Dad, I wasn't thinking of Jonathan. I wondered if you'd let Freddie come and work here with me? Then you and Mum could take days off together. I know she'd like that.'

But Cynthia did not like it at all when Amy explained what she had in mind.

Amy said she knew that rooms above the shop, where she and her brother used to sleep, were vacant now that the family had moved into Primrose Cottage and told her mother she would be happy to accept her father's suggestion if she and Freddie could set up home there together.

'Does that mean you and Freddie are thinking of getting married?'

'No, but we have been talking about living together for some time.'

Cynthia said they ought first to get engaged.

'No, Mum, that's a bit old fashioned these days. We aren't ready to make long term commitments, but we do like each other's company and we want to share life together for a while until we are sure of ourselves.'

Cynthia said she and her father were not yet ready to accept that kind of arrangement, but they would think about it overnight and let her have an answer in the morning.

It was a sleepless night for both parents and time passed slowly as they struggled with the issues involved. It would suit them commercially to have Amy living over the shop and sharing the work load with them, but it would undermine their sense of propriety to have Freddie living with her out-of-wedlock. They liked the lad, and believed he would make their daughter a good companion, but doubted if other people would look kindly on an arrangement which was not yet common practice in the village.

Decision came as dawn was breaking. They had to admit that when they were not much older than Amy and Freddie they faced a similar dilemma. In those days it was unthinkable to discuss such ideas with their parents and they had not waited for the clergy's blessing before putting their affections to the test. The outcome of that test was Jonathan. How much better, they confessed, that Amy had asked permission to do what previously would have been done subversively.

The night before Freddie moved in, he invited the other Banner Boys to a party in the *Perch and Parrot.*

Between libations they shared memories of helping Bernard's campaign against a supermarket and Mathew said he thought it ironic that Bernard should now have turned his shop into a replica of what he had fought so hard to oppose.

'Well, I suppose we've all moved on a bit,' said Billy knowing that Lenny was now working on a farm, Gerald at a Garden Centre, Tommy with the Fire Brigade and Mathew selling computer games. Billy, himself, was about to take over Freddie's job in the public house for he, like Lenny and Gerald, remained true to the country whereas Tommy and Mathew had gone to work in the city.

'It's a pity Freddie's not getting married,' said Tommy, ''cos we could have formed an arch with all those banners we've been keeping. Then he and Amy could have walked out of the church like they do in films.'

Freddie said he doubted if the Reverend Lovelock would have married him, on account of the company he had been keeping. The remark was intended as a quip to relate to his fellow banner carriers, but Dick Perryman, the publican, took it as a reference to people he met in the bar.

Freddie, said the publican, had given excellent service to congregations in the *Perch and Parrot* and deserved a reward from him if not from heaven. He then surprised them all by offering drinks on the house to thank everyone for their custom and to wish Freddie a happy future with his next employer.

A few weeks later, on a warm summer evening, Daphne and Jonathan were sitting under the oak tree where they used to take their fish and chips after a day's work at Blackie's Garage. The old road which Evelyn had uncovered was now fenced off and signposted as of historic interest, but there was no traffic and no tourist to disturb the silence.

'Do you remember when you came to see me in hospital?' Daphne murmured. 'After I fell off Archibald?'

'You were thrown off! It was Archibald who fell.'

'That's as maybe,' said Daphne, not wishing to be diverted, 'but do you remember me saying one day I would teach you something you'd never learn from a computer?'

'Yes, but computers have improved a lot since then.'

'That, too, is as maybe, but I think it's time I started your tutelage.'

Which she did. And her reward came in the following spring, in the form of a curly-headed daughter.

Armed with the example set by Amy, Daphne was able to persuade her parents to let her share rooms with Jonathan at *The Brambles*.

Romance of a less lasting nature occurred for a brief moment at *The Willows*. When Archie heard that the scientists had finished their explorations in Backwater and were about to leave the village he invited Evelyn to the house for a parting drink. Unsuspecting his true motive, she accepted, and was much embarrassed when he asked her to marry him.

'I'm very flattered,' she said, 'but I'd no idea you thought of me in that way.'

'By 'that way' I hope you don't think my interest is only physical.'

'No, of course not! I didn't mean to offend. In fact, I suppose it would have been even more flattering if that had been the case'.

142

Archie *was* now offended.

'Oh dear, I didn't put that very well, did I?'

'Never mind! But you haven't answered my question.'

'Archie, I'm terribly sorry, but there's a very good reason why I can't accept.'

'Is it my age, or is there somebody else?'

'It's not your age. I'm going on another archaeological expedition.'

'With Dr Chalmers?'

'Yes.'

'I suppose I don't have to ask what you will be looking for?'

'That was unkind. If I told you, you wouldn't believe me.'

'Try me.'

'We want to find evidence of other civilisations.'

Archie asked what was wrong with the one they were living in.

Evelyn said that was another question, and unfair to ask an archaeologist.

The new *Village Superstores* was open all week, and one Sunday afternoon, when Cynthia was at the till, a lady who had once been a regular customer walked in.

'Hallo, Mrs Talbot. How are you?'

'Why, it's Mrs Grimley. We haven't seen you in here for a long time.'

'No, I know, but I enjoyed so much coming here when we lived in the village that I wanted to come and say goodbye before we move.'

'I see. That's very nice of you. Has your husband been promoted then, or has he been posted to another store?'

'No. Neither. The company has been taken over by a bigger firm and Arthur has been made redundant.'

When Bernard heard about this he said it was poetic justice, and hoped the new owners would lose their investment now that Backwater had its own Superstore.

THE   END

Author's Biography

Fred Gee grew up in Ilford, Essex, and spent most of his holidays by the River Bure in Norfolk where his mother was born. In the early days of the war he joined the Air Ministry's Meteorological Office, and later flew with RAF Coastal Command as a Met. Air Observer. He was then commissioned, and trained as a weather forecaster. There followed postings to airfields in East Anglia, including Marham in Norfolk. After demobilisation, he graduated with a B.Sc. degree at University College London, where he played an active part in the student dramatic society and became President of the Union. His experience of international conferences while a student led to his being recruited by the Foreign Office, with whom he travelled widely, but he later joined the Rank Organisation and subsequently the British Standards Institution, where he met his wife. There followed many years with the British Film Institute, during which time he took a diploma in management studies. Finally he was made a partner in a firm of consulting engineers and scientists.

Fred Gee served for ten years as a lay member of the governing council at University College before retiring to the country. He is a Fellow of the College, a Member of the Royal Institution, and a Fellow of the Royal Meteorological Society. Married with a son and two daughters, he now lives in a quiet village in Norfolk.